S0-EGP-863

Awakening Of The End

Jeremiah Pouncy

Contents

Title Page

Just A Note Before The Story

Chapter 1   1

Chapter 2   7

Chapter 3   15

Chapter 4   19

Chapter 5   26

Chapter 6   36

Chapter 7   43

Chapter 8   51

Chapter 9   59

Chapter 10   69

Chapter 11   74

Chapter 12   80

Chapter 13   89

Chapter 14   96

Chapter 15   104

About The Author   109

Message From The Author   111

Just A Note Before The Story

In life, there will always be good that is opposed by evil, light that is opposed by darkness. Inevitably, there will be pain felt by individuals that has been and will be felt by everyone in the world. In this society, there are clashing desires, wants, beliefs, and feelings. The one thing connecting everyone is pain. If everyone can sympathize & empathize with everyone else's pain, will there ever be any more conflict? Could there be a person who bears everyone else's pain? All of the agony of defeat… the sadness of loss… the overwhelming negative feelings that build up and block your breathing when you feel those cold tears slowly running down your face… would they be able to push forth and carry the tons of tears and unregisterable weight of the pain of the world. The world may never know, but if someone could, it would change the world. Maybe if their once dormant power has Awoken, they could.

~ JEREMIAH POUNCY

Chapter 1

10:48 AM Tuesday April 13th, 2117

"Y'all going to school today?" yells Iniko as she watches the first match of the South Africa National Hoverboard Competition on her TV in the family room.

"I don't think that we are today," replies Isla as she gets ready for the day. "We already finished our work for the week," she says as she puts on her mascara carefully.

"Oh good job," says Iniko as she is surprised at the fact that they all finished all of their work. "I'm glad that you guys are actually focusing on your classes this semester and not blowing them off again. Cause you know that if you fail a course, that could mess up you guys' credits and graduation time for your under-grad over at Johannesburg Next-Gen U," she says to her younger cousin.

"Yeah, yeah. We know," replies Isla.

School around the world is advancing, along with technology as time goes on. Johannesburg NGU is a college where students can attend class, or not, as long as they maintain a B or above in the class. Isla's best friend, Valerie, is texting her new boyfriend, Amar, while laying in her and Iniko's room.

"Hey Zev?" asks Valerie.

"Yeah," he asks in response to Valerie. "What time is you guys' soccer match today again?" asks Valerie as she inquires about the soccer match that Amar will play in later on in the day.

"I mean, it starts at 4:00 PM, but the players gotta be there by 3:30 PM," replies Zev as he continues to play a game called "Hoverboard Elite 2118" on his new gaming console, the "SquareRing."

"Okay, thanks," shouts Valerie.

"No problem," replies Zev as he stands up.

In the exact moment that Iniko turns off her TV, she hears a chime as her Quadraplex XX gets a text notification from a person named "Atlas". Iniko smiles as she sees the name. As she looks down at her phone, the smile slowly leaves her face as she reads the text, "Atlas: Did you hear about the school system's council all getting assassinated last night on the news?" Iniko replies to Atlas by inquiring more about the situation as she is concerned about the safety of where she lives. Iniko decides to put her phone down after she sends a text to Atlas and turns the TV on to channel 8, "Johannesburg News Daily". As the TV turns on, a news reporter speaks to the news drone and says, "Last night, Monday, April 12th, 2117, every single member of the Board of Education was pronounced dead on the scene at each of their residences. There are no details about their deaths, and a cause of death has not been found."

"Hey, you guys. Did you guys hear about the Board of Education?" asks Iniko.

"Yeah, we heard about it. It is all over everywhere girl," answers Valerie.

"Oh, I've been stuck in this TV watching the Hover-board channel again," says Iniko.

"You always are. Ever since Atlas started teaching you a few months ago, it's all that you watch," responds Valerie.

"Shhh. Don't tell Isla about him. She will be annoying about it," says Iniko as she feels anxious about Isla knowing who she likes.

"My bad girl. I'll zip my lips," says Valerie.

Iniko gets up from off of the couch, and walks outside. She decides to call Atlas. They talk about the recent events and agree to go to brunch at White Fang Diner.

"Oh shoot," Amar says to himself as he looks at his phone after waking up from a nap. The time is 3:08 PM and he hasn't gotten ready for his soccer match today, which happens to be the last game of the season. Amar quickly gets up and puts on his soccer gear.

Amar calls Zev. "Hey Zev. Could you come scoop me up on your way to the game?" asks Amar as he talks to Zev on the phone.

"Yeah that's straight," replies Zev as he gets into Iniko's autonomous car.

He then puts in Amar's address and heads towards his house. When Zev arrives at Amar's place, he watches Amar run out of the door and down the hill with his untied cleats. Zev laughs and rolls down his window as he says, "Hurry up yo."

"Sorry man. I really appreciate it," says Amar as he gets into the car.

Amar & Zev make their way to Loyalty Park and when they arrive, they see their team warming up. "Hurry up you two," says Coach Antonio.

The two boys rush over to the field with their bags and get prepared for their final game of the season. As Coach Antonio recites the starting lineup that he created earlier that morning, Amar and Zev's names are read out loud. They are both excited as they are revved up to be able to start in the final game of the season. Shortly after, the game begins.

At the end of the game, Amar says to Zev, "You played amazing today bro. 2 goals and 1 assist. That's actually amazing man," as they walk off of the field.

"Oh thanks. You too though. I mean you did assist both of my goals and then assist another one on top of that," says Zev as he chuckles.

"Thanks," says Amar as he smiles. "Hey, could I go by your house?" asks Amar.

"Yeah. That's fine by me," replies Zev.

Zev and Amar walk to the car and begin to go to Zev's. When they arrive at Zev's house, Amar goes to Valerie's room.

"Hey Valerie," says Amar with a disappointed look on his face.

As Valerie looks over at her boyfriend, her jaw drops.

"Why didn't you come to my game Valerie?" asks Amar.

"I'm sooooo sorry baby, I honestly forgot," responds Valerie as she begins to get up from her bed.

"Nah. You said that every game this season. Imma go home, but I got 3 assists today. Just wanted to let you know if you even cared," says Amar as he turns away.

"Stop being a baby. You need to get over it. You do this every time. If I say I forgot, then I forgot. It's not deeper than that. Suit yourself though," says Valerie angrily before she begins to lay back down.

"Bye. I love you," says Amar as he walks out of the room and closes the door behind him.

∞∞∞

As Atlas makes his way to bed that same night, he reminisces about his brunch date with Iniko. He climbs into bed as he thinks of how the light shined on her face, making her beautiful skin glow. How her smile shined so bright and white. How her laugh brought joy into his heart. Atlas can't help but smile as he continues to think of Iniko. He wants to tell her how much he's attracted to and likes her, but he never feels like it's never the perfect time. "Well maybe soon," Atlas thinks to himself as he lays in bed staring at the ceiling. His reluctance and hesitation to ask Iniko out leads to a rush of feelings of not being good enough. "Stop being a baby. Stop being a baby," says Atlas as he smacks his cheeks as if he can hit the words into himself. "You can't do anything. You can't lead the basketball team to

Nationals, you're not good at leading anybody. You're not good at teaching Iniko how to hoverboard. You're not even a good friend," says Atlas as he degrades himself as he lies alone in his dark room. "This is why no one can ever rely on you," says Atlas softly as he slowly gets under his dark blue covers and cries himself to sleep.

Chapter 2

9:22 PM Saturday April 25th, 2117

Isla got word of a party that is being thrown at her friend Jabari's house, so she asks Valerie if she wants to go. Valerie agrees to go with Isla to Jabari's house party, so they start to get ready for it.

"What time does the party start?" asks Valerie.

"I'm pretty sure 10, but we can get there whenever we want," says Isla.

"Give me a few minutes, and then I'll get up," says Valerie.

"Yay!" exclaims Isla as she jumps up from her bed.

After confirming the plan to go to the party, Valerie decides to tell her boyfriend, Amar, where she is gonna go. She calls him, and he picks up.

"Hey baby," says Valerie.

"Hey! How has your day been?" asks Amar.

"Good. Isla and I have just been chilling ever since we got back from shopping a couple of hours ago," replies Valerie.

"Awe. That's great. Was it fun?" asks Amar.

"Yes. I got a couple of shirts and pairs of shorts," answers Valerie. "Hey, Isla wants me to go to a party with her, so I just wanted to make sure that it was okay to go," says Valerie as she crosses her fingers.

"Yeah baby, that's okay. Just make sure that you stay safe and that you let me know where you are," responds Amar.

"Okay, I will," replies Valerie excitedly.

"Don't do anything dumb either," says Amar as he laughs.

Valerie & Amar end their conversation, and Valerie begins to get ready for the party. Once she and Isla are all ready, they make their way to Iniko's autonomous car. As they hop in the car and put Jabari's address in, Isla catches sight of a boy who she thinks is in her psychology class. This boy appears to be Geo, and she watches as he passes by her in his car.

"Isn't that the boy in our psych class Val?" asks Isla. "I think his name is Geo or something."

"He runs track from what I know if that is him. That's legitimately all I know about him through. Well, that and all of the girls like him, but he has a girlfriend so you're out of luck," replies Valerie. "But yeah, I think that's his car," she says as she looks out the windshield as the vehicle drives away.

Valerie & Isla then get situated and then hit, "Go", on the car's main screen. The car begins to pull out of the driveway on its own and starts to make its way to Jabari's. The two girls arrive at the house and they see the car from earlier pulling away in front of them. Their car stops in the front of the house. Isla sees the guy walking up the driveway of Jabari's mansion holding a girl's hand.

"Yup, that's Geo," says Valerie as she sees Isla looking his way.

Valerie & Isla proceed to get out of the car and walk up Jabari's driveway. They begin to hear loud music as they approach the mansion. When they arrive at the door, they push it open, and they see people all having a good time dancing and talking all throughout the house.

"Welcome ladies, welcome," says Jabari as he waves his hand inviting them in.

"Hey Jabari," says Isla as she looks at the red cup in his hand. "Where can we get some?" asks Isla as she smiles at Jabari.

"The room on the left, across from the stairs," says Jabari as he laughs and begins to walk away. Isla & Valerie walk down the hardwood floor of the open area and look up to see a beautiful glass and diamond chandelier hanging from the ceiling. They continue to walk down the hall until they reach the room. There are over 20 tables set up with people playing a variety of games from poker, to blackjack, to spades.

Sitting at one of the tables is Geo, who's playing spades, while the girl that walked in with him is talking to her friends. He catches sight of the two girls in his psychology class as they chug a red cup of drink each, and then grab another that they begin to sip from. He doesn't know them personally, so he loses interest and continues to play spades.

The girls begin to roam around the copious number of rooms in Jabari's mansion and talk with their friends from school and work. In the middle of their conversation, Isla feels a bottle of water slap her in the back of the shoulder.

"I'm gonna kill whoever that was," says Isla as she turns around.

When she completes her turn, she sees two boys beginning to start a fight in the area. They were throwing punches back and forth, and one of them was standing by a table with water bottles sitting on them.

"Hey, don't do anything Is-," says Valerie before she sees Isla's Awoken mark begin to glow.

Isla, clearly irritated, begins to summon water from everywhere in sight.

"So you think hitting me is okay little boy," she says as she maneuvers the water to the location of the two guys that are fighting.

With her amazing control of the water, she forms balls of water that she places on the heads of the boys.

"Get this thing off of me," yells one of the boys as Isla begins to laugh at the sight of them struggling.

After realizing that they can't get the water helmets off themselves, they begin to charge at Isla.

"You better go save your friend," says Cleo, who is a mutual friend of Valerie and Isla.

"Yeah," says Jabari as he shrugs. "You are the only one of us that has an Awoken so this is all on you."

"Ugh," says Valerie as she begins to turn her body into diamond and body into rubber.

She runs over to and in front of her friend that is being charged at by two guys that have the aura of raging bulls. The boys throw wild punches towards Isla as she continues to laugh at the sight of the helpless boys. Valerie then extends and wraps her arms around the arms and bodies of the guys tightly to restrain them, and lowers them to the floor.

"Let them go Isla," says Valerie as she turns to look back at Isla who is still laughing.

"Wow that was good. They really thought that I was just gonna ignore them hitting me with the bottle. Ha. You got me f-," says Isla before she is cut off by Cleo.

"You gotta chill with that girl. People are gonna think you're mean and will give you a bad rep for doing things like that," says Valerie..

"Yeah, That's why you can never find a boyfriend. All of em are too scared of you," says Cleo.

"As a guy, I can attest to that," says Jabari as everyone starts to laugh.

Isla gets visibly upset by this since she has always struggled to find love that is reciprocated by the guy that she likes all of her life.

"It's just a joke girl, chill out," says Valerie as she comforts her friend.

"Hey Valerie, did you see Amar's three assists that he got last game?" sarcastically asks a friend of Amar's that plays alongside him on the soccer team. "Oh wait, you're not a good enough girlfriend to even be there," he says as he and his friends begin to laugh as they walk off.

Valerie's arm extends in a split second and connects with the left cheek of the guy, and he drops to the ground as his body goes limp.

"Ugh, I hate that guy," says Isla as she sees Valerie begin to walk away towards the game room.

The night continues and eventually, Valerie starts to talk with a guy that goes by the name of Kel. The room is pretty dark, so she can't see him very well, but she notices that he has an Awoken mark & also that his muscles are abnormally large. They continue to talk for about 30 minutes, and mid-conversation, Valerie asks Kel if he would like to go somewhere more private. Kel agrees, so they begin to walk towards the stairs. As they approach the stairs, Geo and the girl look at Valerie walk up the stairs, leading a guy behind her.

As time goes on, Isla begins to worry about where her friend could have disappeared to. She goes to the room where all of the games are playing to see if Valerie is in there. To her surprise, she feels a tap on her shoulder. She slowly turns around to see the face of Valerie, who has a huge smile on her face.

"Finally I found you. Where were you at girl?" asks Valerie.

"Just catching up with people, but after I couldn't find you, I started to look for you and decided to check in here," replies Isla. "I called you five times Val. Don't ever do that ever again," says Isla as she hugs her best friend.

"I'm sorry that I scared you," replies Valerie. "Well, are you ready to go?" asks Isla.

"Yeah, I got what I needed out of this," replies Valerie.

Isla orders the car to come pick them up and take them home from her phone. Valerie and Isla begin to walk towards the front door to leave as the chandelier from up above begins to fall down from the ceiling. Isla's Awoken Mark begins to glow as she collects water from one of the 50 gallon water dispensers that are lined up in the kitchen, which is across from the game room. The students in the kitchen watch as water seemingly flows like a river past them, and through to the next room. She creates a thick sheet of water in the path of the quickly descending chandelier. Valerie's Awoken Mark begins to glow as well as she stretches her arms around the water and tries to slow down the momentum of the chandelier. The two girls successfully stop the chandelier from slamming into the ground which would have injured many people and damaged the house. They lower the chandelier onto the ground and proceed to leave as if nothing happened. Some onlookers at the party look in disbelief at the fact that Isla and Valerie just used their Awoken's so openly, as most people tend to hide their Awoken abilities. In this world, most of the Awoken abilities are not as strong, or powerful as Isla or Valeries, and people take a strange notice to this. After a few minutes pass, Iniko's car pulls up in front of the house. As they begin to walk down the driveway and get into the car, Jabari pops his head out of the door and yells, "Thanks ladies!"

"The Awoken" has been a phenomenon that began to happen about eighteen years ago at this time. On 1/117th of the population's 20th birthdays, they began to feel marks pulsing and showing on their skin, and they became widely known as "Awoken's". These marks also appeared on other people, seemingly at random, that ranged in age from 20-60 years old. After a few years time, there were developments about the Awoken's. People began attaining faded marks when the day got close to their 20th birthday, and they were able to know what power they would get. People have also begun to be able to determine the power of a person's Awoken mark by the feeling that they get when they are near it. The marks on the body of the users also begin to glow a bright light when they are activated. Each mark has a different design, size, and even color, but they all range in power and fortitude.

Chapter 3

2:48 PM Thursday May 6th, 2117

"Geo is about to run in this 4x100 race," says Layla as she informs Atlas and Iniko about the upcoming event.

"Finally. He's about to dust these people for sure," says Atlas. "Geo is the last leg in this relay for our school," says Atlas as he points to Geo out on the track. "

"Oh okay. That's your friend that you always talk about? The one that grew up on your street and y'all became best friends right?" asks Iniko as she looks up at Atlas who is standing next to her.

"Yeah," says Atlas as he laughs.

"I'm surprised I actually remembered," says Iniko.

"I've only told you about a thousand times," says Atlas as all three of them laugh.

"Shhhhh. It's about to start," says Layla as she taps on Atlas' shoulder.

The race begins and Geo's relay starts out slow. The first runner rounds the corner looking seemingly gassed after just a 60 meters in sixth place. Iniko looks onward, worried about how Geo's relay team will ever be able to pull back this race. When the second runner takes the baton, he trips during the handoff and loses ground which results in the team falling into seventh place. As the team is in sixth place out of the eight teams running, all of the spectators supporting the school, except Atlas and Layla, begin to get a worried look on their face.

"Don't even worry Iniko. Just watch," says Atlas.

Hearing this, Iniko looks left at Atlas, with a smirk on his face, and Layla on her right, who is smiling. As the third person takes the baton with a smooth hand-off, he brings the team into fifth place as he rounds the corner.

"GO GEO!" yell Atlas and Layla in synchronization as they watch Geo receive a flawless handoff.

Iniko watches as Geo speeds past each competitor in front of him one by one until he reaches the finish line, taking first place.

"Yes sirrrrrr," yells Atlas as he raises his hands in the air and runs to the gate where Geo ended the race at.

"He really is as amazing as you guys say he is," says Iniko as she is in awe of the spectacle that she just watched.

"That's my baby," says Layla as she smiles and turns towards Iniko. "I know it's kind of weird to ask, but what are you and Atlas?" asks Layla.

"Well, we're just friends. We're really close though," says Iniko shyly.

"That's not what it looks like to me. Looks like you guys are interested in each other, but you're both scared to make the first move," says Layla as she looks out across the track surrounding the soccer field. "He said you guys went on a date a couple of weeks ago and that it was 'so great'," says Layla as she looks back at Iniko.

"Yeah, I really enjoyed myself too," says Iniko as she

begins to rub her left arm with her right hand.

"It's okay. Just know that I think you guys would look cute together," says Layla as she begins to walk towards Atlas and Geo who are talking about the previous race. "Come on girl," she adds as she looks back at Iniko.

∞∞∞

As night begins to fall, Atlas begins to feel his Awoken mark pulsing as if it sensed that the world would begin to cry soon. "Hm, what was that," Atlas says as he grabs at his Awoken mark as it aches and flashes on and off.

∞∞∞

At exactly 3:00 AM, a very fateful event is about to impact the country of South Africa.

"Yes Mrs. Brown, I can do that for you," says Bunme as Thema Brown, the President of South Africa, asks her to bring her a cup of water. "Hey Pres, I know you've done a lot for me, so I've been taking a lot of massage and muscle therapy classes," adds Bunme as her Awoken mark begins to glow.

"I don't really feel like a massage right now Bunme. I'm sorry, but another time I promise," replies the President in response to Bunme.

"Lighten up Mrs. Brown," says Bunme.

President Brown immediately begins to smile as she

listens to Bunme. "Actually, you can. It'll probably help me out," says President Brown as she changes her mind.

"Yay!" exclaims Bunme as she begins to walk behind President Brown's chair.

"Here, this'll help," says Bunme as she pulls out a syringe and injects a serum into the neck of the President.

"Why'd you do that Bunme," says the President while in a state of shock.

"Cause I'm a member of The Beginning of course. Have fun," says Bunme as she skips towards the door of the room with joy.

"You mean the assassination group that has been causing terror here?" asks President Brown as she begins to feel woozy.

"Yes. What else would it be?" asks Bunme sarcastically. "This is sure to bring pain to everyone who brought pain to us," says Bunme as she closes the door behind her as she exits the room. Once the door closes, The President's Awoken Mark begins to glow.

Chapter 4

3:18 AM Friday May 7th, 2117

"Hello? Hello? I need you all to listen carefully".

"Yo! Get out of my head! I don't want to hear you right now," says Valerie.

"This is Thema, President Thema Brown. I presume that all of you can hear me. As you all may know from the news when I got elected a few years back, my Awoken Ability is the highest level of telepathy. You all may have heard of the group 'The Beginning' and their leader, Ade. They have been planning an assassination on me so that they can disrupt the balance of society and gain control over it...," says President Brown followed by a short pause.

"Hello? Pres?," asks Atlas as he lays in his bed, concerned for the President.

"I'm sorry, I'm fading out. My Awoken Mark is also fading away... I don't know how long I have. My secretary, Bunme, deceived me. After all this time, I never knew that she was a part of The Beginning. She injected me with something and eft me here to die. I'm starting to lose feeling and consciousness. I'm sorry for burdening you five with this. I need you all to look over the information that I have transferred to your minds whenever I go. You guys have had close tabs kept on you by the government because your Awokens have been recognized for their potential ever since you reached the awakening age of 20.....," says President Brown.

All of the students hear her say to herself quietly, "Bunme I can't believe it...," as she tries to speak through the tears.

"I'm sorry you guys. It's just that I've known her for over eight years. I've seen her grow and mature into the beautiful young woman that she is today. And now to be betrayed and deceived by the one that I saw as my own daughter," says President Brown as the tears grow heavier with the building pain in her heart.

Atlas' Awoken sign begins to glow right before he says to the President in an effort to calm her down, "It'll all be okay Mrs., I mean President Brown." He tries to hide the tears as he takes on the President's pain as if it were his own

"Wow. I feel a sense of euphoria. I didn't know it was like this Atlas. You didn't have to do that young man. Thank you for understanding. Um, back to my point, I need you guys to defeat Ade and The Beginning by any means necessary for me...for the world. You guys need to meet at Rocket Park, by the tallest evergreen tree, at 9 AM. It's located about 20 feet East of the swing set, and around 18 feet Northeast of the seesaw. Also, sorry to start your last day of Next-Gen School off like this. I hope that you four can complete your undergrad degrees, and Iniko your PhD program," says President Brown as she struggles to stay awake.

President Brown's Awoken Mark is fading in and

out, the light becoming dimmer with each passing second. "I... wish I could be... you all with this journe.... never.... up..... Together y..... accomplish any...," she says as she loses consciousness and connection to each student one by one.

Atlas continues to cry the tears of President Brown. The pain that he experiences is immense, the pain of losing someone so dear to you. The hurt and agony of betrayal. It's some of the worst pain that he's ever carried. As he lays on his back in his pitch black room, he stares up at the ceiling as tears endlessly run down the sides of his face, Atlas' phone rings. He picks it up, unable to make out the name at the top of his FruitPhone XX.

"Hey. It's Iniko. I just wanted to make sure that you're okay after using your Awoken on Mrs. Brown," says Iniko in a concerned tone.

As he continues to cry he replies, "I'm not really okay, but thank you for checking in on me. I really appreciate it. Don't worry though, I'll be a-okay," as he tries to break a smile through the hurt.

"I'm here for you," says Iniko. "Your Awoken literally fits you so perfectly. From the day I met you, you've always been so caring and willing to carry other people's pain. You empathize and sympathize with them; understand their pain. If everyone was like you, the world would be so much better. Honestly though, I'm just happy that you get something out of it, especially now that your ability has manifested," says Iniko as they laugh simultaneously at her joke.

"I guess. I don't really care for the increase in speed

or strength, or even my Awoken, Lumen, in general. I guess it's cool to be able to manipulate light itself, but it's hard to use effectively. You probably know everything though since you have Shared Knowledge Iniko. Do you think that you could help me out with figuring out ways to use this?" asks Atlas.

"Definitely," says Iniko as she smiles to herself. "It's weird now that I can just touch peoples' heads with my left hand and I can know everything that they do. I get a headache from it honestly, but I do get to know a lot so it is worth it. It just sucks sometimes though because sometimes the books that I'm reading get spoiled," says Iniko.

"True, that could be frustrating. I really appreciate it, genuinely. I gotta go though. Thanks for checking in on me. For real," says Atlas.

"Same here. It is 3:42AM. I'll talk to you later Atlas," says Iniko as she hangs up the phone.

Beep, beep, beep

As Iniko sits on the couch in her living room watching the Hoverboard National Championships with the book "Looping Dreams" beside her on the table, right before the winner is announced and the results are revealed, the channel goes to commercial. A few seconds into the self-driving car insurance commercial, Isla and Valerie walk into the room.

"Ughhh, that thing or whatever killed the vibe of the party," says Isla.

"You're telling me. I almost got a guys' number," adds Valerie.

"Aren't you dating Amar, Valerie?" asks Iniko.

"Well yeah but we didn't do anything. I only talked to him for real. Plussss your little cousin said that it was okay for me to, so teeechnically it's your fault because you should've taught her better," says Valerie.

As Valerie and Isla walk behind the couch and into the kitchen, Iniko says, "You guys are so dumb." She proceeds to ask the two girls, "Did you guys have to use your A.A.'s again at the party too?"

Isla's face turns sour as she thinks back on what happened at the party. She replies to Iniko saying, "Ugh, yes. These two guys were fighting so I took the water from the fridge and splashed them with it all," says Isla. "That was it though."

Valerie looks at Isla and says, "Don't even try that Isla." She then turns to grab a bag of BBQ chips from the pantry as she begins relaying the story to Iniko. "She also manipulated the water into spheres and kept the water on their heads and even laughed while they struggled, so I turned my body into diamond to block the punches coming towards Isla, and restrained the two little boys by turning my arms into rubber. I think that this incident was the one time where using both properties of my A.A. simultaneously was useful," says Valerie as she pours herself a bowl of chips.

"Not again. You guys don't need to be showing your Awokens like that. Everybody does not need to know, especially not now. You guys need to be mindful of stuff like that," says Iniko.

"Okay mom," says Valerie slyly.

"It really doesn't matter," says Isla as she takes a handful of chips from Valerie's bowl.

"Right," says Valerie as she and Isla begin to walk across the back of the couch and up the stairs located behind the couch.

"Go to bed you guys. We got to be at the park at 9:00 AM guys," insists Iniko.

"We are," say Isla and Valerie in synchronization as the two start up the stairs.

"You two have more twin moments than you and Zev, Valerie," says Iniko as she giggles.

"Right," says Valerie as she nods her head as if she wished that Isla was her twin and not Zev.

"Well when you guys fight together, you guys are perfectly synced though. I guess your twin powers show there," adds Isla. "Wait a second, where is Zev?" asks Isla.

Zev hears this conversation from his room, and his Awoken Mark begins to glow. He sinks through his bed as if melting without the puddle, and phases through the floor. He travels through the side of the wall sideways as he looks down at Isla and exclaims, "Right here!"

Isla screams as she drops all of her chips on the ground. "You've got to stop doing that," says Isla, who is visibly upset at her chips falling all over the ground.

"Nah, I'm good," says Zev as he, Valerie and Iniko all laugh.

"9 AM, Rocket Park y'all. Goodnight," says Iniko as she wraps up in her silk blanket, lays her head on her plush pillow, and closes her eyes to go to sleep on the couch.

Isla, Valerie, and Zev all say, "Goodnight," as they all

go to their rooms to go to bed.

∞∞∞

It is 4:42AM when Iniko hears the swift and almost silent footsteps of some familiar feet. She peeks out of her eye and sees the bright glow of a phone shine on Valerie's face as she sneaks out of the house.

Chapter 5

3:28AM Friday May 7th, 2117

At the secret base of The Beginning, there is always commotion and fighting between the members. Bunme is walking down the hallway and into the common room that consists of a large couch facing an 88" 20K Super-Intelligent TV on the left wall, that has her fellow member Nailah sitting on it, alone, watching the Hoverboard National Championships. She sees three more of her comrades surrounding a round table facing a smaller 42" Intelligent TV that had the news of the death of the President, Thema Brown, being broadcasted on it.

"I did that!" exclaims Bunme as she enters the main room that is filled with her allies. "No one can everrrrr step to me again," says Bunme. "My dad can't even," she says as she laughs.

Everyone turns around to look at her but nobody laughs, not even a smirk.

"Don't get ahead of yourself Bunme. Your dad, Ade, leads us for a reason. He's the strongest, wisest, best in everything," says Aren. He looks up to the ceiling as if praising him and exclaims, "Leader Ade!"

"Shut up Aren, you're not even strong enough to be in The Trio like me," replies Bunme.

"No… I just don't need a team and Ade knows I'll be as mighty as him. I mean he is my idol, so if I try and be like him, I'll become just as strong some day," utters Aren as he slowly turns back around in his chair.

"Nah. Get into The Trio with Lulu, Leonel, and I and then you can talk," says Bunme confidently. "All you can do is grow wings, talons, and shoot some stupid feathers," says Bunme as she and the others in the room laugh. "Like what is that supposed to d-," says Bunme before she gets cut off by Mablevi who stands beside Aren at the round table.

Mablevi, the insane escape convict, interjects saying, "I will shape shift my arms into restraints, my tongue into a scalpel, and slowly dissect your entire bodies while I admire the blood dripping along your open bodies if you two don't shut up!"

Bunme's Awoken Mark, Emotion, glows as she softly speaks to Mablevi. The torturous intent that was welling up inside of Mablevi and exuding from him dissipated. Bunme is able to control the emotions of a person that is exhibiting relatively strong emotion just by laying her eyes on them and speaking to them. Nailah continues to watch the TV as she says just loud enough that Bunme and Aren can hear, "You should've let him have at you guys. That would've been a show."

Aren's Awoken sign, Eagle, begins to glow as he grows the talons and wings of an eagle as he speeds over to Nailah from behind. He soars through the sky towards Nailah who sits calmly on the couch, 60 feet away from him. Nailah hears and feels the gusts of wind made by Aren, and she uses her skills from her mastery of Jiu Jitsu and Tae Keon Do to swiftly evade the razor-sharp talons of Aren. Aren soars past Nailah, right over her shoulder, so close that the feathers of his wings brush her shoulder and neck. Aren continues flying clear past Nailah with the momentum that was supposed to collide with her. Nailah quickly leans forward and grabs Aren's right leg and pulls back with all of her power. *Pop* Aren screams in pain as his leg dislocated from his hip. He feels his body change momentum, almost instantaneously, and start flying back towards Nailah. As he looks back to see what is in store for him, he sees Nailah's Flip Flop mark flash. He sees that she had flipped places with Lin, who was at the round table by the TV, and proceeded to grab it and face the wall that is parallel with his body. Her mark flashes for a second time. She swings the TV back as if it were a baseball bat, and when Aren comes in prime striking distance, Nailah swings the TV with all of her power towards Aren's head.

All Aren can do is watch as he sees the heartless and merciless Nailah swing the TV. He stares at the TV as he sees it grow bigger and bigger, until all he sees is black. Aren's wings and talons slowly start to fade away as he lies on the ground with his blood slowly seeping from his head, forming a puddle of dark, crimson blood.

"Pathetic," says Nailah in disgust of the weakness of Aren.

Lin rushes over to Aren to help him out after the exchange. She has gauze, tape and other medical supplies in her backpack. She reaches inside of her bag to pull out the gauze, and she mistakenly pulls out a picture. She turns away from the sight of the others so that they can't see the river of tears begin to run down her face as she looks at herself embracing a young boy with the biggest smiles on their faces. She slowly lowers her hand back in the bag, carefully places the picture into a secure pocket, and then takes out the gauze and tape. Lin's A.A. mark, Call of Plants, begins to glow as an aloe plant begins to grow out of a crack in the floor. She slowly caresses a single leaf and it begins to grow thick with the natural healing ointment, aloe vera. The leaf turns a rich green, like the color of the perfectly green leaves of an evergreen tree. Lin breaks the leaf at the base and slowly massages the aloe vera out of the leaf and onto her hand.

"You shouldn't do that Lin. He deserved it for picking the fight. You saw how I stayed right here," says Bunme.

"Maybe not but he is still hurt so I'll help him," replies Lin.

Lin cleans the blood off of Aren's head, disinfects it with the rest of her supplies, and then places the aloe vera on his battered head with gauze and tape. She then leans his limp body up against the wall so that he can breathe properly and the blood won't rush to his head.

"You'll be healed up in no time," whispers Lin to the still unconscious Aren. "My aloe is special," she says.

Leonel and Lulu walk into the main room and see the scene of Aren propped against the wall, and blood on the floor by a smashed TV.

"Woooaaah!" exclaims Lulu. "What happened?" she asks.

"Nothing," responds Nailah as she turns up the TV.

"Well Bunme, we need you. Your dad has a mission for us again," says Leonel.

"Yay! The Trio is back again! The strongest and the best here! I hate missions that aren't with you guys!" exclaims Bunme in response to the news.

"Right girl!" exclaims Lulu.

Seemingly frustrated by the girls talking, Leonel says sternly, "Just come on you two so that we know what we gotta do."

Bunme, Lulu, and Leonel catch up with what's been going on in their lives since Lulu and Leonel have been taking care of heavier, solo missions, back to back and recently Bunme has missed them. They talk about the different political officers that they have taken out over the past few months as they walk down the long hallway that connects Ade's office and the main room. Leonel talks about having to take out the CEO of Courier Productions, which supplies the country with the large majority of its nanometals which are used in the autonomous cars, TVs, and commercial spaceships. Lulu talks about infiltrating the base of the Wentrol Next-Gen School Headquarters and taking out every person on the Board of Education, which happens to be in Johannesburg, South Africa. School works differently in this time, as students can go to school whenever they please to talk to teachers, but most everything is online. This practice ranges from high school, all of the way to the under and postgraduate levels. Bunme is impressed with the many missions that they discuss. As they talk about their adventures and get caught up, all three begin to smile.

"Took you guys long enough," says Ade as Lulu, Leonel, and Bunme walk into the room simultaneously. "Now that the President is out of the way, we can move forward with the next big mission. This mission is going to be bigger than the assassination of the President so this is why we will need everyone in on this. I need you three to gather intel on anyone in your school system, or young adults that seem to have a strong feel to their Awoken mark. You all should be able to tell the power level and potential of anybody since you guys are all 23 and have plenty experience doing so."

"Whaaat. Why can't Kellan just do it? He always gathers the intel," says Bunme. "I mean, he does have heightened senses, super strength, and can tell power levels at a single glance," she adds.

"Yeah girl. Why can't he just do it Boss? Leonel could just help him stay safe if something happens by using his force fields," adds Lulu.

"You didn't hear? Kellan's mother died yesterday because she couldn't afford the proper health care cause of her job as a nurse and she was all that he had left. He's not able to go on missions right now cause Boss put him on pause," says Leonel.

"Oh, aw man. Well I guess we can just do it then. Hopefully he comes back soon," says Bunme. "I'll check on him later on tomorrow."

"But you say you hate him. Ooookay," says Lulu as she laughs.

"I do, I jus-," says Bunme shyly before she is interrupted by Ade.

"Back to business you guys. Just do what I told you to, and it better be done efficiently and in a timely manner as well. Also, please avoid conflict and altercations the best that you can. Please," says Ade in a serious tone.

Lin walks into Ade's office and tells everybody that Nailah left and she thinks that she is going to spy on her crush Amar. She knows that Amar has been dating Valerie for a couple of months, but she can't get over her obsession with him. He is the only person that she has ever loved & wants to be with him forever but Valerie is in the way of that.

"I hope she doesn't kill that Valerie girl," says Lulu.

"Yeah. She probably will though if she snaps. The pain of wanting something that you can't get is immensely tough to deal with, especially for a hot head like her," says Bunme. "I mean, she shouldn't even be stressing, she doesn't even know the guy."

"True," adds Leonel.

"I told her that she can't or she is out of The Beginning. She has nobody to look at as family other than us since her mom died from cancer earlier this year, and her dad got deported back to Egypt and then died for the very reason that they came here for a few years back, so I know that she won't. She's extremely valuable to us in combat so we can't risk her getting locked up at any cost. Please keep her in check you all," says Ade as he lets out a huge sigh and silence follows.

"Well you guys are dismissed," says Ade. Everyone

begins to turn around and leave until they hear Ade's voice again, "Lin stay here a moment after they leave."

"Okay," says Lin nervously.

The Trio leaves the room and continues to catch up right where they left off. Bunme asks them to remind her about why they joined The Beginning. Lulu tells the others that she joined because her brother got wrongly convicted of a crime and she wants to repay the world for the pain that her brother and she have and have had to experience. Leonel continues after Lulu and says that his family has been treated unfairly all of his life by rich landlords and he wants them and their families to stress and scramble for funds just as he witnessed his mother and father do desperately. By the time they are done with their conversation, they have made it back to the end of the hallway and into the common room again where Aren is now conscious and sitting watching TV.

"Check this out you three," says Aren as he watches the news.

The Trio gathers around the couch and watches the TV as the news of the President is being broadcasted.

"The world cries as the President of South Africa, Thema Brown, dies in her office overnight. The cause of death is unknown at the moment, but there is an investigation underway. The most probable cause is that she was assassinated under order of the group, 'The Beginning', who has been causing terror for this country," says the news reporter as the camera drone rises over the motionless city of Johannesburg.

Back in Ade's office, Lin and Ade continue to have a

standoff in the room. No one has said a single word. Ade begins by saying, "You've been doing well. But with that being said, if you don't do exactly as you're told, I won't hesitate to have my people stop taking care of your sick little brother. One mistake or hesitation and I'll end his life with my own two hands."

"Yes sir," says Lin as she slowly turns around and exits the room as she thinks of her little brother that's dying of an advanced state of a neurodegenerative brain disease called Chronic Traumatic Encephalopathy that is sustained by playing football and taking repeated blows to the head. She knows deep down that the only way for him to have a chance to live is to continue to have Mr. Ade's people at Spylon hospital work on him. She thinks of how she has decided to bring pain to others to save herself from the pain that would be brought upon her by the death of her little brother. "Without the Boss' people's secret techniques, A.A's, and his copious amount of funds, I'll never be able to see him smile again," thinks Lin as she begins to cry as she walks down the hallway.

∞∞∞

As Nailah makes her way over to Amar's house, she realizes that the moon is starting to shine brighter and brighter as she approaches his house. When she gets to the front of the house, she can't see the window so she keeps backing up, slowly, until she can see the room. While she gazes up at the window, Nailah feels rage and pain build up inside of her as she watches the shadows of the sheets rustling in Amar's room window. She leans her back against Valerie's car parked outside, and waits for the movement to stop before she turns around and goes back to HQ for the night.

Chapter 6

8:58 AM Friday May 7th, 2117

The five students: Atlas, 20; Iniko, 21; Zev, 20; Valerie, 20; Isla, 20, are all gathered at Rocket Park as President Brown instructed them to. Everyone saw the news of the death of the president being broadcasted on the TVs when they woke up. The President was said to have been injected with a blend of propofol, pentobarbital, and thiopental by a person in the back of the neck. There were no fingerprints or DNA found on site. She was pronounced dead once admitted into Spylon Hospital. A reporter stated that the President's cabinet, and everyone below, resigned with fear that they were next.

"You guys all looked over the information that we were transmitted right?" asks Atlas.

"For sure," replies Zev.

"I'm still upset about it you guys," says Isla as she begins to tear up.

"Everyone is Isla. It'll be okay, I promise," says Iniko as she tries to console her younger cousin.

"It's been all over the news y'all. People are acting as if there are no rules or laws anymore," adds Valerie.

"Yeah, I saw it this morning too," says Atlas in response to Valerie. "Well just to go over it one more time, the President and her people have been scouting and watching The Beginning for a long time now. Honestly I'm surprised that they have this much information on them," says Atlas.

The Beginning
Objective: Seems to be to disrupt society and cause chaos
HQ Location: Unknown

Member Name	Age	Awoken (No Limits Found)
Ade (Leader)	52	Telekinesis
Bunme (Trio Leader)	23	Control Emotions
Leonel (Trio Member)	23	Create Force Fields
Lulu (Trio Member)	23	Sound Wave Manipulation
Nailiah	21	Swap Places w/ One Thing in Sight
Aren	20	Grow Wings, Talons, and Can Shoot Feathers
Lin	26	Control & Grow Plants Rapidly
Mablevi	28	Shapeshift
Kellan	21	Elevated Senses & Super Strength

∞∞∞∞

Isla gasps after Atlas reads each member of The Beginning's powers.

"You mean the Nailah that everyone says is obsessed with my man? Oh hell no! That better not be her," says Valerie. "This is literally the final straw," says Valerie as anger fills her heart.

Atlas and Zev look at each other with wide eyes as if they know that problems will get started. Iniko tries to calm Valerie down by saying, "It's probably not her girl. You'll be fine."

"Yeah Val. What are the actual chances of that," adds Isla as she leans up against the tree, facing away from the swing set.

"Hey, we should go over each of our abilities," says Iniko excitedly.

"Definitely," agrees Zev.

"I can manipulate water in all states, and that's it," says Iniko.

Valerie proceeds to continue the chain by explaining that her A.A. allows her to enhance her body to take on properties of diamond and rubber in different parts. Zev follows by explaining that he can pass through anything that is in animate. Atlas informs the group that he can harbor the pain of anybody that he chooses, emotional or physical, and can convert it into power depending on the magnitude. He is also able to manipulate light waves.

"I guess it's just me left," says Iniko shyly as everyone's gazes focus on her. "Well I can accumulate the knowledge and select memories of anyone's head that I touch with my left hand."

"Sounds like we have a solid squad," says Atlas confidently.

"Well duh. And the chemistry is great too. We all know each other, well except for you Atlas. Us four have grown up together and now live together in a house we bought after putting money together that we earned from Iniko participating in local hoverboard competitions, and the rest of us having jobs. Also, Iniko said she knew you though and said that you were cool *Whispers* and cute," says Isla as she giggles.

"Shut up Isla. Don't even," says Iniko nervously as Zev, Valerie, Isla and Atlas laugh together.

"Well, anyway, I thought about bringing in some of my people. I don't know if you guys know them, but I'm thinking of my best friend, Geo, he runs track, his girlfriend of 3 years, Layla, and also this guy Amar that I met the other day who I got a feeling will be very powerful when his Awoken awakes," suggests Atlas.

"Hey, we know Amar! He plays on the soccer team with me and he's also dating my twin sister, which is Valerie by the way," says Zev.

"Two months strong baby," says Valerie as she smiles.

"Oh, that's perfect y'all!" exclaims Atlas.

"What can they do though?" asks Isla.

"Their abilities are dormant right now since they are all 19, but once they hit 20 it'll be perfect. They have their marks though, so I know what they will be able to do once their Awoken's awake. Geo will be able to manipulate the Earth, kind of like how Isla manipulates water. Layla will be able to transform into a beautiful being and when people look at her, she will put them under hypnosis while her Awoken is active. And Amar, you guys know I'm guessing," says Atlas.

"Yeah. He's gonna be able to gather moonlight and either convert it into strength, speed, or absorb and re-direct it as a blast," answers Valerie.

"Aye, that's gonna be so cool," says Zev who is vis-ibly excited. "I can't wait for his birthday tomorrow to see what it looks like for real. I wonder if it'll be as amazing as him on the soccer field. He's a literal mon-ster," he says excitedly.

"Wow! Layla and Geo's birthdays are tomorrow and Sunday, so this seems to work out perfectly," says Atlas who has just gained a boost of energy.

"Perfect. And now we have 8 people to combat their 8 members," says Iniko.

"Yup," seconds Zev.

While they all stand by the tree discussing the situ-ation, Zev hears a person approaching the tree. Out into the distance, there is a tall, buff man facing Isla head on. He is walking straight towards her with not a single deducible expression on his face. Isla turns around and faces the man smiling. Zev phases into the tree in wait as he has a bad feeling about the guy.

"Oh, did the sight of me take your breath away," says Isla to the man sarcastically.

The man continues to proceed towards Isla with a gaze of desire for something it seems. As soon as the man is within five feet of Isla, he lunges toward her while cocking his fist back. Isla is stuck in shock by what is happening and all she can see is an abnormally large fist with pulsing veins running up it, through the wrist, across the biceps and triceps, coming straight for her face. She feels what seems to be like a thick rope made of rubber wrap around her stomach and pull her to the side, knocking the wind out of her. In almost perfect sync, Zev phases from out of the tree and throws a powerful uppercut into the stomach of the man. Zev feels his fist hit an object that feels like metal. Out of the corner of his eye, he sees the glow of an Awoken mark.

"Pathetic," says the man as he follows through with his punch into the tree. All five of the students look at the tree in awe as it's bark flies across the park and gets stuck in the metal swing set. They watch as the tree folds and flies into the seesaw, breaking it. While they all are standing there in shock, the man grabs Zev by the throat and lifts him off of the ground. Zev looks down at the man as he struggles to free himself from the death grip of the man's hand. Atlas' Awoken mark starts to glow as he looks at the sight of Zev being strangled by a man who is exhibiting no emotion. The man slowly begins to lower Zev, who is now able to catch a long-needed breath of fresh air. The man slowly turns to Atlas and quietly says, "I'm lost" as he gets lifted into the air by something that looks like an angel to the group of students. Atlas looks up in the sky as the guy slowly rises into the sky, and he sees the man looking back at him. Atlas feels a single water droplet connect with his right cheek, but there were no clouds in sight.

Valerie and Isla run right over to Zev as he continues to breathe heavily as if trying to make up for the breaths of air that he had stolen from him. Atlas sees this image in his peripheral getting blurrier, and blurrier, like a windshield on a humid, rainy day, as he feels a warm embrace from behind. He feels the streams running down his face as his heart aches from the pain, but Iniko's gentle touch makes it a bit easier for him.

Chapter 7

"You're so stupid Kellan," says Aren angrily and he flies towards HQ carrying Kellan with his talons.

"I'm sorry. I don't know what happened. My mind went blank. First my little sister. My mom now. They're both gone. I can't," says Kellan softly as the wind blows the tears off of his face.

"Just take the pain and release all of your anger into your missions," suggests Aren.

"I'm tired of people being able to get away with crime and mischief in the workplace just because they have more money. I don't understand why my mom is able to work at a hospital for 28 years, but can't afford to get treatment when she needs it. It's not fair that no one will care for a person who cares for a person," says Kellan through the tears. For some reason, he looks down at the vast city below him and specifically notices a single park that is under construction that is located by one of his favorite food spots.

"That's why we're in The Beginning right? No matter what we want, we will take it by force man," says Aren while they approach the base.

When Aren & Kellan enter the base, Bunme & Kellan make eye-contact. Bunme runs over to check on Kellan, whom she has grown a liking to. She sees the dried up tears on his cheeks, hugs him, lays her head on his chest, and whispers something as she cries. Her mark begins to glow and Kellan begins to become happy and hug her back.

Kellan walks towards the main room and begins to tell the others that he was on a walk to clear his mind and he passed a group of young adults that each had a high power level and potential. He says that he heard them talking about The Beginning and a few of their powers. Kellan tells his comrades that the only thing he remembers after that, is staring at a young man as he began to be lifted off of the ground as he was overwhelmed by emotion. While he was relaying this information to his comrades, he hears Ade call him to his office.

"I hear that you encountered some students looking to destroy us in response to our assassination of the President," says Ade.

"Yes, and I tried to kill them. My sister, then mom, and now my second family. Not again. Never again," says Kellan sternly.

"You have to be patient. You'll be able to get your revenge on the world soon enough," says Ade. "You're good to go on missions then I assume? Aren said that you destroyed a tree and almost killed a girl and a boy," adds Ade.

"Yes sir," says Kellan.

"Beautiful, your status is resumed," says Ade as a smirk slowly grows across his face. "You're dismissed."

∞∞∞∞

Many hours pass and Atlas, Iniko, Isla, Valerie, and Zev are on their way to a base that was designed for, and relayed to them by the President the night of the assassination. Atlas decides to contact Geo and tell him that he is going to send him GPS coordinates that he needs to meet him at, and to bring Layla as well. Valerie calls her boyfriend Amar as well and tells him to come too.

When the group of 8 arrived at the base, they start to introduce themselves. As they all formed a circle in front of the base, there is a look of disgust that is exchanged as Layla and Isla make eye contact. Zev notices and decides to say, "Chill you guys. You're gonna have to work together, so you guys gotta fix whatever that just was."

The girls look away from each other with the sour look of disgust staying on their faces. Layla says, "You're just jealous that you can't find true love Isla," loud enough that everyone can hear.

Valerie immediately pulls Isla over to her and tells her to just ignore her. Atlas takes the initiative to open the door and looks in absolute awe at the spacious room and next-gen technology for training and intel recording that stands before him. The facility is even better than anyone could have ever imagined it to be. As everyone looks around, they catch sight of tons of live security camera screens, updated gym equipment, and even training spaces and equipment for every Awoken

Ability that was known for the group.

Geo says, "Yoooo this is so tough!" as he steps into the humongous base and looks all around him.

Zev agrees and says, "RIGHT," as loud as he could. The students are standing just inside of the entrance of the base as they hear the echo going on, and on, and on.

"We even got beds," exclaims Geo as he runs down the right balcony of the base past each room.

"Everyone in separate beds tonight please you guys," insists Iniko.

"Yeah, please," says Atlas while he slowly walks down the stairs to the bottom floor as he looks around at the impressive facility.

As the students continue to look around the base, The Trio begins their mission to scout out and gather information on their enemies. They track them back to the base, but they haven't acquired any more intel than that, nor do they know how to enter the base.

"I think learning that they have 8 members and knowing the location of their base is good enough, don't you guys think?" asks Bunme.

"Yeah, this is straight," replies Leonel.

"Cool, cool. Let's get back to HQ then," says Bunme.

While the Trio is walking back to HQ, they see their comrade, Mablevi, pinned on the ground by the police with Awoken disabling handcuffs around his wrists restraining him. Leonel is the first one to start running over to the altercation.

"He's always the first one to try and save one of us isn't he," asks Lulu even though she already knows the answer.

"Yeah, he sure is," replies Bunme.

Lulu and Bunme start to run, lagging a bit behind Leonel, towards Mablevi. Leonel's Mark begins to glow as he approaches his friend. Leonel scopes out the area. He first notices an alleyway about 20 yards away from Mablevi that can be used as an escape route. He sees that there are four squad cars with 2 officers standing outside of each car with guns pointed at Mablevi as he struggles to escape. The one officer on top of Mablevi is a big, 210 pound officer, the only one that looks like he can pin down Mablevi.

Leonel's Mark begins to glow as he approaches his friend. He creates force fields and pushes all of the police and vehicles back with them. The sirens of the vehicles silence as they all break from the impact of the force fields. Bunme and Lulu's Awoken marks start to glow as well as they get closer to Mablevi. Bunme yells to Mablevi to calm down while he is still fighting to break the restraints. Her voice does not reach Mablevi as he continues to struggle to break free. Leonel dives and tackles the officer that is on Mablevi's back. At the same time, Lulu speeds the sound of Bunme's voice up and amplifies it so that it reaches Mablevi sooner and has more effect. Without this he may have gone insane and self-destructed while trying to shapeshift constantly while he had on the special handcuffs. Leonel places a force field around Mablevi so that the police couldn't get to him. He also places a force field around himself and the officer that he tackled so that it'd remain a one-on-one fight. The cop pushes Leonel off of him and Leonel hits his head on the force field.

"Ow man. Don't you know that these things hurt," says Leonel to the officer while he rubs his head.

Leonel notices that the officer is unlatching his gun. He immediately lunges towards the cop and punches him with his right hand.

BANG

"Sorry sir. You're gonna need some better aim than that next time to get me," says Leonel as he elbows the cop's head repeatedly. "Look what you did. It's getting a bit messy in here," says Leonel, to the unconscious cop, as he looks around at the blood that was splattered across the force field and sidewalk. "Probably gonna leave a stain. All your fault sir," he says as he uses the body of the bloody officer as a crutch to help him get up.

As Lulu and Bunme approach the force field protecting Mablevi, Leonel manipulates it so that there is a hole for the two to enter through. Bunme & Lulu enter the force field and Bunme proceeds to pull out a master key for the special handcuffs.

"How do you have that Bunme?" asks Lulu.

"My dad gave it to me because Mablevi is an escape convict, if you didn't know," answers Bunme calmly.

"Um... well now I'm uncomfortable but okay," says Lulu in a shaky voice.

"He's cool with us Lulu, chill," says Bunme.

Bunme releases Mablevi from the restraints and he stands up while rotating his arms and wrists, slowly regaining the lost feeling in them. Lulu calls to Leonel, telling only him the plan that her, Bunme, and Mablevi have made. Mablevi shapeshifts into an armored car, and Lulu and Bunme hop in. Leonel releases the force field, and the three members of The Beginning swing by Leonel's force field. He hops in and Mablevi speeds off with a loud *skrt* by the tires as they try to get a grip on the road. They speed away from the scene and turn down the alleyway.

∞∞∞∞

As night begins to fall, Atlas decides to go on a little walk outside to clear his head as he begins to feel a bit overwhelmed. He starts to talk to himself out loud as he walks down the street that he grew up on. "Am I really good enough to do this, to bear this weight? Am I really strong enough to be the backbone for so many people. It's just so… so hard," he says as he tears up. He slowly squats down as the gentle breeze blows against his skin. He looks down at the ground in front of him as tears slowly began to roll down his face. He slowly looks up at the dark, cloudy sky. "I don't know if I can do this. I don't know if I'm supposed to wield this power. I try, I really do, I want everyone to be happy at the end of the day. I wish that I could just make everyone's pain disappear. I…," he says as he starts crying heavily.

Geo steps out of his house for a breath of fresh air. He looks down his driveway and he sees his best friend since they were eight and nine years old, bawling on the sidewalk all alone. He starts to tear up at the sight of Atlas, who he sees as an older brother, crying so heavily. He begins to walk over to Atlas.

When he gets to Atlas, he stands right in front of him and says, "Get up bro."

Atlas slowly stands up and places his forehead on Geo's shoulder as he continues to cry.

"You're the best man I know bro. Caring, kind, respectful, and the greatest friend that a person could ever have. You are way more than enough man, you're the best," says Geo as he holds his best friend as the clouds start to part, and the light of the stars begin to illuminate the sky.

Chapter 8

12:01AM Saturday May 8th, 2117

"Happy Birthday Layla and Amar," exclaim the other six people in the group as they all stand inside of the base.

"Thanks you guys," says Layla with a big, beautiful smile on her face.

"Yeah, thanks for real," seconds Amar who smiles shyly.

"Well what are y'all waiting on?! Let's see your Awokens!" exclaims Isla. "So who's gonna go first?" she asks.

"Well I gotta go to the bathroom real quick, so don't start without me," says Geo as he runs to the bathroom.

"Ladies first," says Amar.

"Aww, what a gentleman," says Layla as she winks at Valerie.

"I'll kill this b-," is all that Valerie can say before Isla splashes some water in her face.

"Chill out girl. She's just acting childish. Stop feeding into it," Isla tells Valerie.

As Valerie and the others go to the open field, Geo comes running out of the bathroom. With everyone gathered around in a semi-circle around Layla, she starts to activate her Awoken and her mark begins to glow. Her hair starts to grow longer and her eyes glow a bright white. She looks at the feet of each person around her until she gets to Amar's. She looks up and into his eyes, and his eyes begin to form a red ring around their iris'. Layla makes him bow down to her while he is under her hypnosis which pisses off Valerie, but she is able to reserve her thoughts for now.

"Wow, that was so cool," exclaims Isla. "Do it to me next Layla!"

"No, we gotta see Amar's now," says Iniko.

"Yeah. It's past midnight so the moonlight should be good for Amar's first go at this," adds Atlas.

The group goes outside to test Amar's new Awoken power now that it isn't dormant anymore. Amar's Awoken sign begins to glow as a light purple tint, presumably the moonlight, surrounds his arms and legs. With each passing second, the moonlight becomes a darker purple.

"Hit something," yells Geo.

Amar proceeds to concentrate all of the moonlight into his fist and strikes a 200 pound, stone boulder outside of the base with a right hook. The boulder looks completely unaffected by the punch, with not even a speck of dirt or dust falling off of it.

"HA! Your punch did absolutely not-," was all that Geo could say before he gets stopped mid-sentence as Iniko smacks him in the back of the head with her left hand.

At this moment, the boulder starts to glow. "Everybody watch out!" yells Atlas.

Everybody, but Iniko, turns and looks at Atlas, then

back at the laminating boulder. A tear slowly rolls down Iniko's cheek, in which she quickly wipes away. She sees the memory of Geo watching Atlas cry and hearing what Atlas said and it hurt her heart. The boulder continues to glow even brighter, and brighter, and then explodes without making a single sound. Amar slowly looks down at his fist, and then slowly looks back up to see everybody staring at him with every single one of their jaws dropped.

"I don't know what to say," says Amar nervously in reaction to his new power.

"YOU'RE SICK!" exclaims Geo.

"For real though," says Zev.

"I read about a Lunar Eclipse happening Sunday night, so your powers are going to be even more amazing I bet," says Iniko with a hopeful sound in her voice as she informs the group.

After they talk about the spectacle that they just witnessed, the group makes their way back inside to eat some cake. Everyone is getting to know each other even more and enjoying themselves. Iniko tells the rest of the group that she needs to step outside for a second for some fresh air. Everyone continues to talk, and Valerie, Amar, Zev, and Isla all walk downstairs to the self repairing training field to fight for fun, and to try out new ideas and tactics.

Iniko let's out a huge sigh as she looks into the dark, endless forest stretching wide in front of her. She hears the base of the door open and turns around to see Atlas walk through the doors.

"Follow me," says Atlas as he gently grabs a hold

of her hand. "Now I know that it's Layla and Amar's birthdays today, but I wanted to do something special for you. You always take care of everyone in our group, and I appreciate how you're always there for me," says Atlas as he guides Iniko up the stairs on the side of the base that lead to the roof.

Iniko is caught off guard as she looks at two chairs and a table set up perfectly, with the brightest yellow roses, carefully placed inside of an exquisitely beautiful white and black embroidered vase, and the most ripe strawberries that she has ever seen in her life. Iniko starts to tear up as she remembers telling Atlas that her favorite color is yellow, and that her favorite food ever has always been strawberries, the first time that they met a few years ago. Iniko asks Atlas what all of this is for.

"This is for being my favorite person to talk to on the phone, see, hear the voice of, any of that, ever since I got to know you some years ago. I wanted to ask you out formally. I had to make it special and I hope it's not so much that it weirds you out. And I-," says Atlas until he feels the soft, warm caress of the familiar hand across his cheeks as he feels his face being pulled slowly downwards.

Iniko and Atlas share a passionate and love filled kiss on the roof of the base. Iniko chuckles and tells Atlas, "Of course I want to go out with you dummy. I was starting to think you'd never ask."

"Well here, to make up for the wait, I have a surprise for you," says Atlas. He guides Iniko over to the left chair and she sits down, facing the vast, dark green pasture and trees out in front of her. She looks up at Atlas and looks him in his eyes. She hears Atlas say softly, "Now close your eyes." Ten seconds pass, "now open."

Iniko opens her eyes to see a beautiful image of the African Savanna all around her. She looks to the left as she sees deer eating berries from a bush, while a family of elephants are walking past them. She looks right as she sees the tall figure of a giraffe eating leaves off of the top of a tree. She feels her body become filled with emotion and tears begin to drip from her cheek, down to the ground as her cheeks become flushed with the happiest smile a person could ever have.

"This is so amazing Atlas," says Iniko as she looks around in awe. "I never knew you could do this," she says as a tear filled with happiness and joy begins to slowly roll down her cheek.

Atlas smiles with all of his bright, white teeth showing and proceeds to say, "I've just been practicing with my Awoken of manipulating light and light waves a lot lately. It was extremely hard at first, but I just had to keep at it. I don't think this is anything really special, but I'm happy that you seem to like it. It makes me feel a bit better that you do," says Atlas as he looks from Isla, and out at the sight of his beautiful creation.

"Atlas, you started off not even being able to alter the light waves around that basketball that your dad gave you a few months ago to make it look brand new. Now this Atlas, wow. I know you may not be able to accept it, but this is amazing Atlas. You need to give yourself more credit," says Iniko as she looks up at Atlas.

"I guess you could say it's a little bit special," says Atlas as he feels a feeling of admiration of his work well up inside of him. "I just wanted to see you smile and not as stressed as usual. You feel just like everyone else," he says.

"You can always be humble, but at the same time be able to recognize the time, effort, and quality of something that you did. You're truly amazing Atlas," says Iniko as she looks out at the Savanna again. "This is truly extraordinary and beautiful Atlas, truly," says Iniko as she soaks in the magnificent sight.

Atlas and Iniko spend a little bit of time alone while the younger ones are all inside having fun. While they are outside spending quality time together, an unforeseen divide is about to start making its way into the group.

Layla calls Aren over from the field to where she and Geo are sitting. She begins to tell him about a party that her and Geo were at a few weeks ago, in which they saw Valerie talking to a guy.

"Well I know that she talks to other guys, that's a given," says Amar.

"Yeah, I know, but the thing is... she went into a room with the guy," says Layla reluctantly.

"And the guy is talking about what happened on social media," says Geo. "I really think that you should talk to her about it man. Honest."

"Oh...," says Amar softly as his vision begins to get blurry. "Well, okay... thanks for the birthday gift."

Then Amar goes home for the night, nobody notices him leaving, not even Valerie.

About a half hour later, Iniko and Atlas go inside and tells everyone that it is time to get some sleep for the night. Isla notices that the two of them walked in holding hands and yells, "Uh oh! New couple added to the gang!"

Everyone starts to laugh at the sight of Atlas and Iniko quickly releasing hands as if they weren't holding hands before. "Maaan, hold her hand," says Geo as he laughs.

Then, everyone went to bed in the base for the night. Everyone except Amar.

$\infty\infty\infty$

As Amar walks home, he thinks to himself, "She never would have done that. I know my Valerie. I shouldn't even be getting upset because I know that she didn't, she would ne-," he says before he stops in his tracks.

Amar hears a rustle in the grass. He turns to the left and catches sight of a shadowy figure in the trees along the side of the sidewalk.

"Hey kid, you have a powerful aura to you. We could use you," says the shadowy figure.
A business card is thrown at the feet of Amar.

Amar bends down to pick up the card and reads it. It reads, "The Beginning, Meet @ Pilot Park at 11AM by the longest bench."

"You have three days to decide. I'll be there those three days. You won't find me after," says the shadowy figure as it fades into the darkness of the forest.

Amar calls to the woods, "What if I don't know." There is nothing but silence. Amar hears no sound except for the gentle draft of the night winds. He looks at the card once more before he puts it into his jacket pocket. Amar continues on his journey home, clutching to the card while thinking heavily to himself the entire walk. When he arrives at his house, he decides that he will ask Valerie about the cheating rumors tomorrow, and that he will keep the strange encounter a secret.

Chapter 9

1:42 PM Saturday May 8th, 2117

Isla wakes up everyone in the group so that they don't waste too much time. "Wake up!" she exclaims.

With everybody now awake, they all get ready and go down to the main floor of the base.

"Woah, check out the dope table guys," says Zev as he runs towards it like a kid that just saw a jar of candy.

He looks down at the table and tells everybody to come look at it. Atlas leads the rest of the pack down the stairs to see the table that Zev is so excited about. When they all reach the large circular table, Iniko taps it. The table reads, "Read message from President Brown", "2 Days Ago". Iniko taps the button labeled "Open".

The table reads out loud, "In 3 days time, you all must meet at this table. Make sure you are all within the circular line drawn along the blue tile floor, in white, when the clock hits 12PM. Thank you, President Brown."

"So that's tomorrow guys. Make sure you tell Amar, Valerie. I haven't seen him this morning," says Atlas.

"Okay, I'll tell him the next time that I see him," says Valerie as she worries about the whereabouts of her boyfriend.

"Well I guess that's all that we have to do guys," says Geo.

"You guys have to be on time. Seriously you guys," insists Atlas.

"We will," says Iniko in response to Atlas as she grabs a hold of his hand.

"For now, everyone can do their own thing I guess. I'm gonna go downstairs and train in the Room of Lights, but you all can do as you please," says Atlas. "Oh yeah, I thought of creating a group name, and also designating a leader."

"Hey, I've got one that I've been thinking about actually," says Geo. "Well since we have to defeat The Beginning, how about we call ourselves 'The End'?!"

"You know what, I'm not even gonna argue it this time," says Valerie. "About the leader though, I feel like we should wait until we see what we have to do tomorrow."

"That's fine by me," agrees Zev.

Everyone else in the room agrees with Valerie's idea and that is what they will do. The door of the base opens, and Amar walks just a single step inside of the door. He asks Valerie if he can speak to her outside for a minute and she agrees. As they walk outside, Valerie can tell that her boyfriend, Amar, was upset just by looking at him. She has known him for four years before they started dating this year so she knows how he is.

"What's wrong babe?" asks Valerie.

"I've just been hearing things that are being said by some people... rumors specifically. They're centered around you, so I wanted to come to you before I assume anything because I trust you wholeheartedly. But um... about that party you went to the other day... I was told that you did some stuff with a guy that was there. I just want you to be honest with me right now Val, even if it'll break by heart," says Amar reluctantly.

Valerie sighs when she hears the words that Amar speaks to her. She starts talking while she stares at the feet of Amar. "To be honest with you, I never meant to hurt you or cause you any sort of pain. When we got in that big fight the other week... and we didn't talk for a few days... it made me want to get back at you for it... for making me cry. I know it was dumb. I know it was and I am very sorry Amar. With everything in my heart, soul, and mind I promise that I will never d-," says Valerie before Aman interrupts her.

Valerie sees raindrops fall from the sky and hit the ground in front of her, one after another. Her head slowly rises until she looks at Amar's face. He has tears running down his face as his heart feels like it has been getting squeezed harder and harder with each passing second. He tells Valerie, "Thank you for being honest, but that is all Valerie. We're done," as he turns away from her to start his journey back home.

Valerie continues to say that she is sorry to Amar, but all that she can do is stare at the back of the boy that gave her his all to make her happy, slowly fade away into the distance as the tears got heavier, and heavier, making the saddest sight of her life become blurrier, and blurrier.

Inside, Atlas wonders what was taking Valerie and

Amar so long to come back in so he asks Isla, "Do you know what's taking those two so long?"

"No," replies Isla. "They're probably just messing around or have made their way to someone's house at this point. It has been a while," adds Isla.

"True," says Atlas. "Isla, Zev, and Iniko, do you guys wanna go get some food?" asks Atlas.

The four of them agree and begin to go and get some food. At the same time, as if it were fate, three members of The Beginning were leaving their HQ as well.

While walking down the road, Kellan, Lin, and Aren discuss where they are going to eat at. The block has a park that is under construction on one side and restaurants on the other side with lots of people walking. There are also a few fights going on between people with different views on what to do since the President has passed. Kellan's Awoken mark begins to glow as he sees familiar figures, smells familiar smells, and recognizes some power levels that he has encountered before.

"It's them again. Those are the people over there," says Kellan as he points towards Atlas, Zev, Iniko, and Isla, who are walking to their favorite restaurant, Gresco's Vegan Diner.

"No point in wasting time," says Aren as he shrugs his shoulders. Aren's Awoken mark begins to light up as he begins to grow wings.

Out of the corner of his eye, Zev sees a feather flying extremely fast, heading straight for Isla's neck. He grabs a hold of Isla and his Awoken mark glows as he phases himself and Isla to avoid the shot as Atlas and Iniko keep walking ahead, oblivious to what had just occurred. Zev taps Atlas and Iniko on their shoulders and explains to the two of them what had just happened. Atlas' Awoken starts to glow as he bends the light around himself and his friends to make the group invisible to others.

"Some interesting Awoken's we have here," says Aren. "Let's play with them."

Atlas turns to see three people walking towards the park. Iniko chimes in, "I think that those people are members of The Beginning guys. There was a person named Aren that could shoot feathers. Along with that, the only way that they could've spotted us is if one of them had heightened senses, or something of the sort, which the person named Kellan has. He also has super strength if I remember correctly."

"Yeah, that's right," says Atlas. "We have to go confront them. This may be a very impactful move for us that could help us tomorrow."

"We could see how we work as a team now since we've been training too," says Isla.

"Well, I guess we can do that. I'm useless in combat though you guys, so it's basically going to be a 3v3," says Iniko reluctantly.

As the group of four walks over to the park, the three members of The Beginning go over their strategy to take on The End.

Atlas and the others arrive at the park and they see two men and a woman, all with their Awoken marks glowing. They witness a woman that has a ring of plants around her, a man with wings and talents, and lastly, a man in regular clothes that has almost inhuman arm muscles.

"I can smell you guys so there's no need to hide! Also my name is Kellan," shouts Kellan in a confident manner.

"I'm Lin," adds Lin.

"And I'm Aren, and we are a part of The Beginning if you were wondering," says Aren.

Atlas bends the light around Isla as she builds a six foot deep water hole trap. When she comes back near the group, he reverts the light from directly around them back to normal, but he manipulates the light around the park to make it look like nothing is happening to the outsiders.

The group of students introduce themselves and they are ready to go at any time. The shadow of the tree behind them begins to grow bigger and bigger and begins to cover them. As they turn around, Aren yells, "GOTCHA", as he flies directly towards Zev.

Zev turns around and begins to run towards the ever growing tree behind him.

"I imagine that that is what Kingsley would look like if he has the chance to get older. He reminds me so much of him when I see his face," Lin thinks to herself as she stares at Zev.

Zev phases through the tree and underground.

"Nice one kid... but running does nothing," says Aren as he redirects his aim into Atlas.

Atlas grunts as he feels the hard wing of Aren's collide with his rib cage. Atlas drops his right arm around the head of Aren, which is pressed up against his side. He then proceeds to grab his right wrist with his left hand, and pull up with all of his might in an effort to choke Aren. Aren doesn't even budge as he stays on course until he runs Atlas into the metal fence surrounding the park.

"Atlas," yells Iniko as a look of worry comes across her face. She then feels her feet get tied up in vines coming out of the ground.

Isla begins to run towards Lin and Kellan who are standing in the center of the park. Isla's Awoken mark starts to glow as she begins to summon water from the pipes that run underground. She creates a trident out of the water and begins to fight Kellan with it. They are fighting and are seemingly evenly matched in terms of brute strength.

"Tie him up Lin," yells Aren.

Lin proceeds to wrap vines hanging from the tree around Atlas, tying him to the fence. Aren begins to fly towards Isla with his talons pointed at her with a demonic look on his face. Out of nowhere, Zev phases from underground and uppercuts Aren, stopping him in his tracks. Aren winces in pain as he falls to his knees, and then gets kicked directly in the chin by Zev. Then Zev phases underground again. Isla knocks Kellan backwards with a combination of blows that she created during her training at the base. While he is unbalanced, she creates a wave of water in the air and knocks him back even further. With the distance between them set up perfectly in favor of her, and Kellan trying to regain his balance, Isla begins to throw her trident with all of her might in the direction of Kellan. As she's releasing the trident, she feels a knife stab her in her calf, and it causes the trident to slip out of her hand at the last possible second of the release. Isla looks back and notices that there is a feather in the back of her leg. She then turns to look at the trident that is now soaring through the air heading straight for Iniko, who can't move a muscle because of the vines tying her feet to the ground.

"Noooooo!" yells Atlas as he cries at his inability to do a thing to save the girl that he cares most about.

The trident is flying at 40 mph, aiming directly at Iniko's chest, and she all but accepts her fate. Out of the blue, Zev's head begins to rise out of the ground, followed by his body, and finally legs, right in front of Iniko. He turns around and smiles at her as the trident closes the distance on striking him through his back.

"Tell your cousin that I love her, and have for the past seven years," says Zev as tears run down his face.

As he closes his eyes to accept his fate, Atlas' Awoken mark begins to glow even brighter as he starts to cry after taking all of Zev's pain away. He rips through the vines as if they were made of paper. Atlas begins to stand up and run straight for Iniko and Zev as tears fly off of his face as he runs as fast as he can. As he runs, Aren shoots a feather into Atlas' foot which causes him to stumble. As he is falling over, he begins to do a roll to maintain his momentum.

BOOM *WHOOSH*

The sound of the trident striking a body is all that Atlas hears as he is mid-roll. He looks up to see a woman standing in between him and Zev who is standing in front of Iniko.

Zev turns around and opens his eyes as he feels the wind from the trident's momentum being stopped by something. He looks into the eyes of Lin as she smiles and falls into his arms with the trident struck through her, running through her back and out of her chest, with blood dripping off of the tips. "You remind me so much of him. It would've been like witnessing him dying with my own very eyes right in front of me," says Lin quietly to Zev as a single tear slowly runs down her check, as all of the plants and vines all slowly died along with their keeper.

In a flash, Aren flies over to Kellan, grabs him, and flies away into the clouds up above. Zev then looks in front of him as a picture hangs off of the end of the trident of a little boy hugging the woman laying in front of him. The only thing that the group can do is sit in the park in shock, no one moving a single muscle as the city continues to move all around them. Atlas' Awoken mark continues to glow as he hides the debris and remnants of the battle.

∞∞∞∞

Amar arrives at a house party at 10:18 PM that

night. He wants to clear his head and distract himself with whatever he can. As he is trying to enjoy the party, he makes eye contact with a girl that he finds very attractive. She also keeps staring at him, so he presumes that a conversation between the two of them would go well. He walks over to her and they start to talk. The two of them are hitting it off, and some time passes as they listen to the music and dance. After talking for a little while longer, Amar asks the girl if she would like to go to a room. She agrees and as they walk up the stairs, Amar can only think of distracting himself from missing Valerie. When they arrive at the room door, Amar opens the door for her. She walks inside of the room, and he slowly follows her inside, closing the door behind them both.

Chapter 10

The next morning, Amar wakes up and gets ready to begin his venture to Pilot Park. As he walks down the road, he sees everything moving as if it were a simulation. He observes the cars zooming by taking people to their destinations, couples talking and smiling with the happiest of looks on their faces, and little kids playing with their Augmented Reality Battling Pets, Fighting Forever Pals. He walks down the road passing the sign labeled "Pilot Park" as he sings the song playing in his headphones. He looks in the distance and sees a man in an all black tracksuit sitting in the middle of the longest bench in sight. He looks down at his phone to see what time it is. The time reads "10:58 AM" and thinks to himself, "Well that's gotta be him doesn't it".

He walks over to the man and sits beside him. Amar hands the card back to the man and says, "I'm in."

"So you came. We're glad to have you," says the unknown man.

As Amar and the man begin to walk into the forest behind the bench, the man begins to speak, "The name is Leonel, one of the members of this thing called 'The Trio' in our organization. It basically just means that we are the best, and strongest, team in The Beginning." He looks over at Aren who is right beside him, walking with a determined look on his face and says, "To be completely honest though, with your potential, you may be able to take one of our spots though if you really try hard enough throughout your missions."

"Cool, cool," says Amar. "I'm ready for my first mission. I have some built up emotion and anger that I need to let out. Someone close to me caused me the worst pain that I have ever experienced in my life, and I will not stop until I make everyone feel what I've felt, the pain of betrayal. I must deceive my victim in the worst, most painful way that I can. I will do this."

"Lemme guess, a female broke your heart?" asks Leonel.

Amar continues to look forward and walk alongside Leonel as he doesn't say a word.

"Well, you don't have to tell me. But everyone here has experienced immense pain and we are all here together, so we can be your new family. We're sometimes rough with each other, but it's all born from the connection that we have that brings us together, pain from how the world is today," says Leonel as they approach the HQ of The Beginning.

Amar and Leonel walk inside of the base, and into the main room. Amar recognizes the hair of somebody sitting on the couch, but he doesn't mind it as his heart has become ice cold... for now.

"Guys, this is the new recruit, Amar," says Leonel.

Everyone turns from where they are sitting, or standing, to look at him. Amar scans the room, and he sees a familiar face to go along with the hair that he had seen earlier. The girl that he was with at the party last night was in the very room in which he stood in. He can't take his eyes off of her, and Leonel takes a notice.

"Hey Nailah," says Leonel.

"What do you want Leonel," replies Nailah in an annoyed tone of voice.

"This guy won't stop staring at you. I don't know if you guys know each other or what, but you can show him around cause I picked him up," says Leonel as he goes to talk to Lulu, Bunme, and Kellan at the round table.

Amar walks over to Nailah and they make eye contact. Neither of them decide to speak on what happened in the room at the party last night. There is an awkward silence as Amar can only look at her as if he fell in love at first sight.

"Well hey. Say something," says Nailah.

"Um, hey. So about last night... it was fun. I really enjoyed spending the night with you," said Amar shyly.

"Yeah, same here. Just a quick question, are you still dating Valerie?" asks Nailah.

"No, and there's no chance for us to get back together either. I'm done with her. I want something new," says Amar.

Nailah looks away from Amar, "So that's why you're here, huh. She broke your heart and you want to take it out on the world," she says. "I figured that was why you were at the party."

"Yeah. But my heart is gone now, so I'm going to make everyone feel how I feel, however I can," replies

Amar. "So this room is all that there is to this place?" asks Amar as he scopes out his surroundings.

"No. Well kinda. I mean, the Boss' office is down that hallway over there, but after that... well then actually... that is it," says Nailah as she points to the hallway leading to Ade's office.

Everyone looks to the ceiling as they hear a noise being made from somewhere inside of it.

"Everyone, come to my office," says Ade on the intercom.

"Who knew that we had one of those," says Leonel, causing everyone to laugh.

Everyone in The Beginning's HQ gets up and makes their way down the hallway. As they get to Ade's office, they all line up one by one, horizontally, in front of him.

"Your biggest mission yet starts today. All of you guys will be going on this mission all together and it will determine the future of us. If you all can't pull this off, then we're done. You guys better not slip up," says Ade as he slowly pans his eyes across the room. "I assume that not all of you have heard of the news that Lin died yesterday in a battle," he adds.

"Wait what did you say? Lin died?" asks Lulu.

"Yes. I was there when it happened," adds Kellan.

"She went up against those people from 'The End' and lost her life, but Aren and Kellan luckily made it out alive. They are strong you guys, so don't underestimate them just because of their age or lack of experience or complete nonexistence of intimidation," warns Ade.

"We got it boss. We will be careful, and also complete the mission in a timely manner. We've heard it a million times," says Mablevi.

"Talk back to me one more time and I'll send you back to prison Mablevi," says Ade sternly as he stares deep into the soul of Mablevi.

As the clock approaches noon, Ade begins to tell the members the details about the mission that will decide the fate of the future of The Beginning.

Chapter 11

10:59 AM Sunday May 9th, 2117

As the group begins to get ready for the big day, they decide to eat breakfast as a collective. Zev decides to create his own special blend of potato salad for the group for their big day. Little do they know that this is the last bit of joy that they will have for a while.

"This is sooo bad," laughs Atlas as he tries to eat some of Zev's potato salad that he made for everybody for breakfast.

"Aw come on," says Zev.

"I was kidding man," says Atlas as he eats more potato salad. "This is actually really good."

"Yeah for real Zev. This bangs," says Geo as he stuffs his mouth with the potato salad.

"Why don't you ever make this at home Zev?" asks Isla.

"I never feel like cooking when I get home from soccer practice during the week so I don't," replies Zev. "Do you even know how to cook Isla... NO. I didn't think so," says Zev as he looks at Isla with a straight face.

"Geez, I was just asking," responds Isla.

While Zev continus to make breakfast for the group, everyone keeps on talking and enjoying each other's company, everyone except Valerie. When Iniko notices that Valerie hadn't said a single word this morning, she asks her, "How are things with you and Amar going?"

A look of sadness comes flush over Valerie's face as she informs the group of what happened. Everyone is surprised by the news and can't believe a single word that they just heard. Isla didn't even know about anything that happened.

"You didn't even tell me girl?" asks Isla knowing that her best friend didn't say a word about anything and hid the secret from her as well.

"No. It was a mistake that I made and I didn't want to even talk about it. And now I've lost my boyfriend, who was also my best friend," responds Valerie as she begins to cry.

"So that's where Amar has been," says Atlas. "I felt that something happened, but I never could have imagined that it was to this magnitude."

As the group continues to talk about Amar and Valerie's ending, they eat the food that Zev has prepared for them. During a pause in the conversation, Atlas goes over to the oven and pulls out a cake labeled "HAPPY 20TH BIRTHDAY GEO! Love, Your Forever Friends From The End" and then places it in front of Geo. As they all proceed to partake in the cake that was made for Geo, Geo steps on the ground as his Awoken mark begins to glow. With the impact of his foot hitting the floor, a pillar of rock rose from the ground, and up to the ceiling.

"That's so dope baby," says Layla as she looks at her

boyfriend in awe.

"Oh my goodness Geo!" exclaims his best friend Atlas.

"Our team is going to be literally so amazing now," exclaims Zev as he continues to stare at the pillar with wide eyes and a look of excitement on his face.

"Thanks guys," says Geo as a gigantic smile grows over his face. "I couldn't sleep last night because I knew that my Awoken would awake at midnight. I just tried many different things like," he says as a block of Earth rises from the ground. Excess dirt falls off as it slowly takes shape of a large wooden axe and he grabs the handle and says, "this."

Everyone's jaw drops as they witness the fascinating display of new power that Geo just put on so calmly. Everyone is extremely happy for Geo as he explains his power some more to them. He also says that he thought that they had forgotten about his birthday last night, but everyone reassured him that that is not the case.

As everyone is continuing to talk and enjoy themselves, the clock on the large table displays "11:55 AM. Beginning Protocol Sequence" across it. Everyone looks down at the table as it begins to flash a bright white off and on. An audio recording begins to play from the speaker in the table saying, "Hello you all. The is President Thema Brown. I have pre-recorded this message for whenever the time comes. Today you will be going on your sole mission to defeat The Beginning."

"Everyone, make sure that you're in the circle," says

Iniko as she looks around to make sure that everyone is in the circle.

Everyone steps inside of the circle to make sure that they are in position as the table told them to do when they read the message the other day. At the exact second that the clock reads "12:00 PM", the audio recording begins to play again. "Today you all will be battling against The Beginning in a series of events. The outcome of these events will determine the fate... the future of South Africa," says President Brown on the recording as a large, circular glass cylinder with no bottom drops, covering the group.

"Woah hold up man, this isn't what's supposed to be happening right now," says Zev now concerned.

Everyone begins to look around as the cylinder that they are enclosed in begins to drop into the floor. The audio recording starts up again and they can see the table sink into the ground as it continues to say, "You all will be taking on The Beginning in a series of game competitions today. The ultimate winner will be determined by who wins the series that is in a 'Best 2 out of 3' format."

The group all looks at each other as all they can do is listen and look at each other as their fate is being determined by a table.

"This is some BS," says Layla under her breath.

"You guys will start with a game of 'Capture the Flag', in which you all will be placed on one side of the arena with a flag at the top of a ramp on your end. The Beginning will have the exact same setup on their side, parallel to you all. The arena will be an expansive field with no roof to allow nature to play a factor in the games. There will be a river running along the right side of the arena, and the games will take place at night, but of course there will be lights illuminating the space. The objective of this game will be to retrieve the flag from your opponents' base and return it to your base. Any type of fighting and use of Awokens are both permitted. There are no rules in any of these competitions, meaning that killing is permitted, and causing death or injury is unpunishable during these games," says the table, causing the group to have worry and anxiety come over every one of their hearts and becomes visible on their faces as well.

Nobody in the group can utter a single word as they continue to listen to the table talk. There is a slight moment of silence. "Hello you all," says a voice unknown to the group. "My name is Ade, and I'm the leader of The Beginning. My people will be taking you all on to decide the fate of our world. To be honest with you all, we have kidnapped the President for our own reasons, and led the world to believe that she is dead. In reality though, she is still here. I mean, we couldn't just kill the President and that just be the only fun that we have," says Ade as he laughs demonically. "I struck a deal with the President after my beautiful daughter, Bunme, put her in a medically induced coma. My people over at Spylon Hospital did such a wonderful job didn't they," says Ade as he laughs. He continues, "The deal was that she would assemble a team of the strongest fighters that she could, and they would be pitted against my squad. If her team wins, we will release her and disband The Beginning as a whole and do as you all say. If my team wins, on the other hand, I will be continuing to scheme against this country and create an avenue for hurt people to cause chaos to this society secretly. The stakes are so high! I absolutely love it," says Ade as he starts to laugh diabolically. "Well that is all that I have to say to you useless people. My people will come at you with the intent to kill, and also will use any means necessary to win. So yeah, try not to die," says Ade as he laughs to himself as the audio recording ends.

Isla continues to have haunting flashbacks from the sight of her trident being struck through Lin. She remembers last night, the countless times that she continued to wake up crying and gasping for air, as the nightmare of what occurred the day before replayed in her head. "I can't. I killed somebody. I didn't mean to. She didn't do anything wrong and she was hurting too. I heard what she said. I'm sorry. I deserve pain. I'm sorry," Isla remembers her voice saying as she cried through the night. She remembers hearing footsteps walk toward her room, seeing a light glow, and then falling asleep as she felt relieved of her inner demons that were causing her pain.

Chapter 12

9:48 PM Sunday May 9th, 2117

As The End approaches the arena near the start time of the games, they begin to talk about their plan for capturing the flag. Their cylinder is positioned behind their flag, overlooking the arena out in front of them.

"Before we go, I think we need to decide who will be our leader. I personally think that Geo should be our leader, as he can rev up our energy, and also can lead us in the journey to capture The Beginning's flag. He will also most likely run with it since he is the fastest in our group," suggests Isla.

"I agree," says Zev.

"Well what about Atlas?" asks Valerie.

When Atlas hears Valerie's comment, he starts to think of himself in a leadership position and believes that he can't do it. "I can't do this. I'm not good enough to carry everybody on my back. I won't be able to do anything good," Atlas thinks to himself.

"Oh, no. I believe that Geo is best fit for this job," says Atlas as he redirects the attention off of himself.

"Well I guess that's decided then," says Iniko.

She wants to push Atlas and try to get him to be the leader, but she remembers tapping into Geo's memories as they watched Amar's powers the other night, so she did not push it.

"Let's go team. We gotta protect each other and get this flag no matter what, the world literally depends on what we do right here tonight guys. I love y'all. Let's go!" exclaims Geo as he tries to motivate his team as the doors to the arena open.

The groups hear a loud buzz project through their rooms and the arena.

"The time is now 10:00 PM..... GO!" blasts the speakers in the room of the arena.

As The End begins to walk through the doors, Atlas' Awoken mark begins to glow as he manipulates the light to hide and disguise the flag. Zev, Valerie, and Iniko start to run down the ramp connecting the platform and ground, and straight towards the flag on the other side of the arena. Zev then phases underground to stay out of the sight of the enemies. Geo starts to run across columns of Earth that he summons from the ground that rise above everybody else. Layla and Isla start to make their way up the right side of the arena as they see a river running all along the side.

On the opposite end of the arena, Amar begins to make his way to the right side of the arena alongside Leonel. His arms and legs begin to take on a strong purple glow. Aren, Kellan, and Lulu's Awoken marks simultaneously begin to glow as Kellan and Lulu begin to run down the ramp, towards the middle of the arena with Aren flying above them. Mablevi and Nailah slowly begin to walk down the ramp, and to the left side of the arena.

The two groups heading straight for the opposition's flags meet at the middle of the arena. Valerie and Iniko stop as they see Aren, Kellan, and Lulu approaching. Kellan senses Zev coming up from under the ground. As soon as Zev tries to surprise Lulu from behind and hit her, Kellan instinctively turns around and throws a kick directed at Zev's face, but Zev evades the blow and phases back into the ground. At this exact moment, Valerie's Awoken Mark begins to glow as she stretches her left arm to wrap around the wings of Aren to bring him down. Then around Kellan's body and arms while he takes his eyes off of her to deal with Zev. Aren sees Valerie's arm fly towards him and he moves out of the way just in time. She succeeds in wrapping up Kellan and pulls him to her. The elasticity of the rubber is in full use as her arm snaps right back to her, lifting the helpless Kellan from the ground and towards her. Valerie turns the rest of her body into diamond and prepares a punch for Kellan that he will take as he flies towards her.

Aren determines that the only way to stop her fast enough is to shoot her with a feather, so he launches a feather at Valerie's chest. Lulu also sees that her comrade, Kellan, is in trouble, so she redirects the sound from Geo's Earth manipulation to try and disrupt Valerie's plan. As Kellan flies towards Valerie as her arm retracts, she unleashes a brutal punch to the face of Kellan, in which he becomes incapacitated. The sound waves from Lulu then blow towards Valerie and the arrow lands in the ground. Zev witnesses this as he phases back up from under the ground and puts Lulu in a chokehold. Iniko runs to Zev and lays her left hand on Lulu's head and retrieves all of the information that she can about The Beginning and their plans to win the game from her. Zev continues to squeeze harder and harder until Lulu's body goes limp. As Aren witnesses this happening, he shoots a couple of arrows and retreats by flying to where Leonel and Amar are.

"Lulu and Kellan just got taken out by this girl who could use her body like rubber and some extremely hard material. It looked like diamond but I'd hope that that was not the case," says Aren as he flies above Leonel and Amar, matching their pace.

"Wait, you said a girl that can manipulate the properties of her body man?" asks Amar.

"Yes man. It was crazy," replies Aren.

"I'll take care of her," replies Amar as he runs towards the middle of the arena in which he saw Aren fly from.

"The only thing that we have going in our favor is that Nailah has used Flip Flop on the Earth guy who was on the rock pillars, so she is making an easy way to The End's base. Also Bunme has the Earth guy stopped right now by making him feel overwhelmed and tired," says Aren to Leonel as they continue on to the opposing base.

Zev drops Lulu on the ground as she loses consciousness and then runs back towards Iniko and Valerie, who is now on the ground. Iniko tells Zev and Valerie that The Beginning plans on having Amar sneak around their right side of the arena to retrieve the flag, and then run back to their base with Leonel who will protect him.

"Wait. Amar?" asks Valerie.

"Yes," replies Iniko.

"I'm gonna go and help out the others over there," says Valerie and she runs to the left. "Make sure to tell Atlas what you told me you guys. Iniko you go, and Zev, you go and capture the flag," says Valerie as she runs away.

"Dang it Val," says Zev as he phases back underground.

"Yup," replies Iniko as she lets out a sigh of relief as she begins to run to tell Atlas about The Beginning's plans.

Amar and Valerie run towards each other unknowingly, Valerie hoping to see the one that she lost, and Amar to see the person that he still truly loves. As they approach each other, their runs ease up into a walk as they each catch the sight of their best friend.

"Hey," says Amar nervously.

"Hey," says Valerie as she steps closer to him extending her arms.

Amar pushes her away softly

"Oh," says Valerie as she looks down at the ground. "I didn't mean to... No. I won't make any excuses. I'm sorry Amar. I understand that you may never forgive me, but I don't want to lose my best friend," says Valerie as a tear slowly runs down her face.

"I don't want to lose you either Val," says Amar as he walks up to Valerie and wraps his arms around her. "I don't believe that I'll ever forgive you for what you did to me, and I won't say that it's okay either. I'm not saying that we're getting back together because that most likely will never happen, but I don't want to lose my best friend either," says Amar as a tear drops on the head of Valerie as if the pain connected the two of them.

"I'll try and understand you better to make this better for both of us and I will be here for you with whatever you need me for," says Valerie.

"Okay thank you. I really hope that you can grow and mature and become the amazing wo-," is all that escapes the mouth of Amar as he feels a sharp object break through his back, grab his heart, and squeeze it til it bursts like a water balloon filled with blood.

As a blank stare lies on the face of the lifeless body of Amar, his eyes are still fixated on the one girl that he has ever truly loved in all of his life. His dying wish to be that she can grow and become even better than he believes that she can be. His body slowly falls to the ground like a cooked noodle would. Valerie stares straight ahead at a man that looks insane as he laughs with an arm that looks like a grappling hook with blood dripping off of it. The grappling hook retracts and reverts back into a normal hand and arm. The man slowly tilts his head to the side and laughs while he says, "He thinks he can talk, hug, and cry with an enemy. I will kill someone before they do that. And now you're the next to die little girl."

∞∞∞∞

Atlas feels a wave of pain pulsing in his Awoken mark. He activates the mark and he sees pain being harbored by everyone in the room as if it is being exhibited by them. When he looks across the room one more time, he sees one undeniable image, the image of Valerie exuding an immense aura filled with the sadness and pain from losing a loved one. Atlas thinks to himself who could have been hurt that would cause Valerie that much pain. "Amar?" Atlas asks himself.

As Isla and Layla sit and wait by the river, they see Atlas running extremely fast through the middle of the arena and then making a sharp left turn.

"I wonder what that was about," says Layla.

"Yeah. He only runs like that when he sees someone in trouble," adds Isla.

Atlas runs over to Valerie as fast as he can after seeing her pain. When he runs up behind Valerie, he slowly eases up his run as he sees an insane man laughing as he stares at Valerie, who is looking at Amar's dead body in front of her. "What happened here," asks Atlas as his Awoken sign begins to glow.

"I killed him of course," says the insane man. "My name is Mablevi. You may have heard of me. I made a name for myself being referred to as 'Mablevi the Mass Murderer' a few years back," says Mablevi as he laughs to himself.

Atlas slowly begins to feel his body overload with

strength, and a slight tint of a bright white light begins to surround his body as he absorbs the pain of his comrade and experiences his own pain on top of that. He begins to slowly walk towards Mablevi, who shape-shifts into a 7 foot tall robot with a machine gun as one arm and sword as another.

Valerie witnesses her friend Atlas move so fast that it looks like teleportation, right in front of the robot that is Mablevi. He sinks his fist deep into the core of the robot. The robot slowly shrinks back into Mablevi the human, and he coughs up blood.

"Don't you dare hurt my friends or cause them pain. You don't have the right to murder anybody or cause anybody that type of hurt. You should have loved everybody and understood that the same way you were hurt, they have been to. You don't have to take it out on everyone," whispers Atlas into the ear of Mablevi, who has laid his chin on his shoulder.

The tint to Atlas' body began to slowly rise and fade away into the atmosphere, as did the life force and pain of the killer Mablevi.

∞∞∞∞

On one end of the arena, Zev phases out of the ground, retrieves the flag of The Beginning, and phases back underground. A few minutes later, on the opposite end, Nailah is making her way down the final Rock pillar steps that Geo created. She approaches the flag and tries to grab it, but it confuses as her hand doesn't touch a thing but itself. She looks around and there are multiple flags, all created by the light manipulation of Atlas at the early stages of the game. As Nailah tries to figure out which flag is the real, tangible one, Zev phases out from under the ground and places the flag down at the base and The End gets one game.

Speakers turn on

"1 point to The End. The score is now 0 The Beginning - 1 The End"

Both teams return to their bases and relay to the others what all has happened since they were all last together. Everybody was extremely shocked and upset after the death of Amar is revealed.

"The next game will start at 10:48. You have a ten minute rest, so use it," shouts Ade from over the speaker.

Chapter 13

"The next battle is 'Castle Invasion'. The End will be in a base that is manufactured to be indestructible and houses a chest that needs to be opened by The Beginning, and opposingly, defended by The End. The time limit on this match is 1 hour and 30 minutes. There are four entrances to the building, but only one leads to the treasure room. Just like the first game, anything goes. Mablevi and Amar both died in the last match if you would like to know. Nobody will be tried or charged for a crime for the deaths of them either," says Ade over the speakers in the waiting room.

As Ade is explaining the next game, the two groups can see the arena completely flip over. The new floor has a building in the center of it with 4 entrances, one in each direction (N, S, E, W). Each team delves into their plans as they start to get set up for the match. "Participants to your spaces," says Ade and everyone in The End walks down the ramp and into the house to set up. The Beginning stays in wait outside of the house: Aren at the East entrance, Kellan at the North entrance, Nailah at the South entrance, and The Trio at the West entrance. The End sets up inside of the house placing Geo in the Treasure room, Isla & Zev in the East room,

Valerie in the South room, Atlas in the North room, and Iniko & Layla in the West room.

"The time is now 10:48 PM. START!" exclaims Ade over the speaker.

Everybody from The Beginning rushes into the rooms. In the South room, Nailah runs into Valerie and the door behind her closes.

"Really. What is my luck," says Nailah as she scoffs at the sight of Valerie.

"We can fight if you have a problem with me girl. I don't even know you. Never seen you in my life," says Valerie as she begins to get agitated.

"My name is Nailah. Does that ring a bell?" asks Nailah sarcastically.

Right as Nailah finishes her sentence, Valerie begins to run at her and her Awoken sign begins to glow as her fists change to diamond. Nailah quickly turns her back to Valerie and when she is 3 feet away, her Awoken mark flashes, and she switches places with Valerie. Valerie is caught off guard as she feels like she has missed something that has happened and looks at the closed door in front of her. Nailah then jumps on the shoulders of Valerie and begins to put her in a triangle choke with her legs. She wraps her right leg around Valerie's neck, and her left leg over top of it. She then proceeds to squeeze them around her neck and flexes as hard as she can. Valerie struggles to stay up and begins to stumble until she ultimately falls over, not being able to maintain her balance. Nailah continues to choke Valerie until her body becomes limp and she stops trying to struggle. Nailah then goes to check if the door won't open and it won't. She's in the wrong room.

"Ughhh!" exclaims Nailah as she punches the ground.

∞∞∞∞

As Isla and Zev lie in wait for their opponent to appear, Isla informs Zev that she needs water. Zev let's her know that he has a spare water packet in his shoe for emergencies and gives it to her.

"You're so weird for having this, but you are a life-saver Zev," says Isla as she lets out a sigh of relief.

Zev smiles as he phases into the wall that is aligned with the door that their opponent will come in through.

Aren comes flying into the room with his Awoken mark glowing and feathers coming straight for Isla. As Isla manipulates the little bit of water she has, she re-directs most of the feathers. She gets cut by a few, but she thinks that she did good for what little water that she has. As Aren flies through the door, Zev phases through the wall and punches Aren in the exact spot that he had kicked him in at the park. Aren's wings slowly fade away as he drops to the ground.

"Really Zev," says Isla, upset. "I needed to get him back for the park," she says.

"No you didn't. Just like Atlas says, "Just because someone causes you pain doesn't mean you should do it back. Try and solve problems with the least amount of pain on both sides possible, and sympathize and empathize with one another. That's what's best because you never know what someone's situation is, or past experiences are," as he imitates Atlas.

They both laugh as they think of Atlas telling them these things during breakfast that morning.

∞∞∞

In the North room, Atlas awaits his opponent. In front of him appears Kellan.

"Oh, it's you again," says Kellan as he lays his eyes on Atlas. "Hopefully this is the last time I ever have to see you."

Kellan begins to run towards Atlas and they begin to exchange blows repeatedly. A left hook from Atlas connects with the rib cage of Kellan. Kellan replies by throwing a two punch combo to the mid section of Atlas. They exchange jabs, hooks, and kicks to all parts of each of their bodies. While this exchange is going on, Atlas begins to feel an aura of pain spreading throughout the atmosphere and gets an uneasy feeling. As they continue to fight, Kellan begins to get fatigued and misses a right overhand in which Atlas counters by grabbing the back of his head, and driving his right knee into Kellan's forehead. Kellan's skull has a visible dent in it, and is also losing a lot of blood.

"I hope more of your friends die," says Kellan as he begins to fall over and pass out from the impact and loss of blood.

Atlas' Awoken mark begins to glow as he begins to shine a bright white, substantially brighter than when he confronted Mablevi. In the moment that the light began to surround Atlas, he closes his eyes. He opens his eyes and turns towards the chest room. He begins to lift his foot and punches through the before said "indestructible" wall and a loud sound goes off as he witnesses Bunme open the chest and wink at him.

BUZZZZ

"1 Point to The Beginning. The score is now 1 The Beginning - 1 The End," says Ade over the speaker.

Atlas watches as Iniko gets dropped on the floor by Leonel who was strangling her and she proceeds to gasp for air repeatedly. He also sees Layla propped up against the corner with her head hanging as she appears unconscious.

"Good try kid. Now pick up your bi-," says Leonel before Atlas flashes right in front of him and stares into his soul which catches him off guard. Atlas then turns to pick up Iniko, who now has a red mark of a hand around her neck from Leonel, and begins to bend over to help her. She tries to tell Atlas something while pointing to the West room as tears stream down her face, but the words are inaudible.

"Don't forget your other friend either," says Leonel as he turns and starts to walk into the West room. He walks steadily behind Bunme and Lulu as they walk towards the door of the West room. "For real, check in here man. I left you a gift," says Leonel as he walks out of sight.

"They don't call us The Trio, the best in The Beginning, for no reason buddy," says Bunme.

Atlas walks towards the room that Leonel, Bunme, and Lulu are passing through. He looks around the dark, West room and he can't see a thing. The exit door begins to open and light seeps in from outside. The room slowly fills with light and it uncovers a horrific scene. There are lights hanging from the ceiling by a few wires, shooting sparks everywhere. There are many spots of blood on the walls, ceiling, and floor that has been splattered. Atlas looks all around the room and when he is almost done scanning the room, he sees his best friend from childhood, Geo, laying on the floor dying from his fractured skull, ribs, and spine. He has a large puddle of blood surrounding him as Atlas calls out to him as he looks in disbelief and terror, "Geo," says Atlas.

As if the pain of watching his best friend die wasn't heavy enough for him, he absorbed all of Geo's pain so that his friend could pass pain free. Geo slowly opens his eyes and slowly moves them to look at Atlas, as he can't move his neck or body at all. Atlas continues to see Geo's pain exuding from his body as if the scene wasn't enough to know. Geo can only say, "Tell Layla I'm sorry... that I wasn't strong enou... and that... that...I love her...please," before he coughs up more blood. "I lo... I love you... bro...," says Geo as he passes away from his injuries.

At the sight of this, Atlas begins to cry and cry as his body becomes deeper and deeper cloaked in light as his Awoken mark glows. Iniko looks around the corner to see Atlas crying tears in four different streams without making a single sound. It seems to her that the pain and hurt in Atlas' face would never go away. She describes the scene of Atlas crying as an island in a sea full of tears.

After some time passes, Atlas is taken out of the room by security guards that Ade hired to help out. Atlas' body seems lifeless as he gets guided back to the waiting room. While on the way back to the waiting room, Iniko sees Atlas in the distance being guided by security guards as he looks like a walking dead man. She runs to Atlas and hugs him from behind. The security guards split off and go their own way when they see Iniko holding Atlas.

"You'll be okay Atlas. I'm right here for you baby. I understand how you feel," says Iniko as she squeezes Atlas as tight as she can.

She holds onto him as tight as she can as if to never let go. Atlas begins to feel the pain slowly leaving his body and the light surrounding his body begins to slowly dim.

Chapter 14

12:48 AM Monday May 10th, 2117

"Since the battle score right now is tied at 1-1, we will have to proceed with the most entertaining and brutal competition. This final match will be a 'Survival/ Death Match' in which each team will fight in a team battle against each other until one team has all of their players either knocked out or deceased. The security drones will carry away anybody that reaches one of those conditions so that there is nothing in the way of the brawling. Again, anything goes, and the winning team will have what we agreed on at the beginning carried out," says Ade with an excited tone of voice.

The waiting rooms with each team in them slowly slide down the ramp and onto the empty arena floor. As the containers slide down, The End starts to discuss how they will defeat The Beginning.

"I know that we are hurting, I can see it, I can feel it you guys. With that being said, I don't want anybody to take out their frustration and anger on these people. All of them are experiencing pain and I feel it every time my Awoken activates. I know everybody is hurt by the loss of Amar and Geo, but we have to be able to under-," says Atlas as he gets interrupted by Valerie.

"No. No. I will cause them all the pain that has been

brought upon us," says Valerie as she cries about losing Amar

"Yeah, we have to. They killed Geo," says Layla as she cries about losing her boyfriend.

"I understand you guys. Just please try you guys. What good are we if we do the same thing as them. I'll lead us this time. I believe I got it this time so please believe in me," says Atlas as he tries to smile through the pain.

"I believe in you Atlas so I'll ride with what you said," says Zev as he pats Atlas on the back.

"Let's go with what Atlas says guys. He'll be our leader now, so we gotta follow what he says," says Iniko.

"That's cool with me," says Isla in response to her older sister.

As the cylinders approach the halfway point in the middle of the arena, they start to slow down until they come to a complete stop. Isla begins to look around as she and the others step out of the room, and notices that there is a pond in the back right corner of the arena, and she takes a note of that. Each team is directed by Ade over the speaker to line up along each wall. Once everyone is ready and set, "FIGHT," yells Ade from over the speaker.

Everyone's Awoken marks begin to glow as they start to walk toward their opponents with a desire to win for all of the motivations in each of their hearts.

Aren begins to soar up above everybody and creates a shower of feathers that rain down on The End. Zev phases underground and begins to travel behind The

Beginning. The Trio breaks off from Kellan and Nailah as they head straight for Valerie. Valerie, Layla, and Atlas head straight for The Trio, as Isla and Iniko head for the others.

As the duo from The End begins to run towards Kellan and Nailah, Aren swoops down and picks up Iniko from the ground and flies into the air. Iniko begins to scream and throw her body around in an attempt to escape the razor sharp talons of Aren.

"Shut up. Stop being annoying and difficult," says Aren as he looks down at Iniko.

Iniko continues to fight with Aren to try and break free. Aren lets out a huge sigh as he drops her from about 20 feet in the air. Iniko screams as she free falls down, all up until the moment that she hits the ground. Her legs bend the wrong way, and she is knocked out by the impact of hitting the ground.

As security drones start making their way to the arena field, everyone looks to see what they are going towards. They slowly pick up the broken Iniko, and proceed to take her into a sky box room at the top of the building.

As Atlas sees this, his Awoken sign begins to glow and he begins to gain a white aura around him again. He looks over at Iniko being carried away, and then back at The Trio. He begins to run at 35mph towards them, and Leonel throws up a force field in front of The Trio as they set up for the altercation that is soon to commence. Bunme and Lulu hide behind the force field as they watch Atlas run straight at them.

While this is going on, Nailah's Awoken begins to

glow as she switches places with Isla. Isla is stunned by what has happened, but is able to think of what she needs to do. Kellan starts to throw a punch at Isla, and his Awoken mark begins to glow. Isla manipulates the water from the pond and forms a shield to defend against the punch. The water of the shield absorbs most of the impact, but Kellan's fist sinks into the water a little bit. As Isla sees Kellan's fist stop moving, she freezes the water around his fist and he falls forward because of it. The weight of the ice around his fist feels like a ton as his Awoken mark fades away because of overuse and a large amount of stress to his body over the past few days. Iniko then manipulates more water into a hammer, freezes it, and hits Kellan in the head with it. As she follows through with the swing of the hammer, Nailah comes flying towards her head with a flying kick. At the exact same time, Aren is diving down to take out Isla. The two members of The Beginning collide and their bodies go limp as they lose consciousness because of the impact.

"Well that was close," says Isla as she wipes the sweat off of her face.

Isla begins to gather more and more water as the drones come to recover Aren and Nailah. Unknown to her, a fight is about to go down about 30 feet to the right of her.

Atlas' Awoken mark begins to glow as he braces for impact with the force field (you have this word together and sometimes spaced). He lowers his shoulder as if he was playing football, and follows through into the force field.

Leonel says, "Woah there," as his feet dig into the ground as he gets pushed back by Atlas.

Atlas begins to absorb everybody's pain, all up until Bunme's Awoken mark begins to glow as she says, "Calm down now. Become confused."

Lulu's Awoken Mark begins to glow as she directs the sound around the force field and into the ears of the increasingly powerful Atlas. Atlas immediately stops in his tracks and looks around him at the vast space in the arena. "What am I doing?" Atlas asks himself.

"Well you're trying to go home and the door is over there," says Leonel as he points behind the confused Atlas.

"Oh, thank you sir," says Atlas as he turns around and begins to walk towards the wall.

"Stupid," says Leonel as he lunges at Atlas like a tiger.

Before Leonel can tackle Atlas, Zev phases up from out of the ground and throws a clean left hook into the face of Bunme. As she falls over now unconscious, Lulu looks at the body of her friend fall over. Lulu begins to scream and she amplifies the sound all around her and it throws Zev off guard. Atlas also begins to turn around as the effects of Bunme's Awoken ability fades away as he hears the scream. He sees Leonel in slow motion, lunging towards him. He watches as he sees a block of water, incoming from his peripheral, wrap around the head of Leonel and shift his momentum away from Atlas. Then right behind Leonel, a block of ice slams into the side of the head of Lulu. Lulu begins to wobble like a penguin until she finally falls flat on her face right in front of Zev who is sitting on the floor. He slowly leans backwards until he is lying on the floor and spreads out his arms like a plane. "Gosh I'm exhausted," he says as he falls asleep. Atlas looks over towards Isla and sees a man with a block of ice as a hand, standing behind his friend. As the drones pick up Zev, Bunme and Lulu who are all now unable to fight, Isla is standing off her guard watching the showdown unravel. Isla slowly looks at the ground as she sees the shadow of a figure get bigger as if it was right behind her, then everything goes black.

Atlas witnesses the image of Isla being knocked out by Kellan, and slowly dropping to the ground. As this happens, Atlas begins to run towards Kellan, but with the first step, is tripped by Leonel. Atlas quickly catches himself from a complete fall and recovers. He reaches Kellan quickly and they fight, quite similar to the round before. Kellan isn't as strong now, so he is slowly getting pieced up by Atlas. Atlas parries a jab thrown by Kellan and then completes a strong right hook into the side of Kellan. He then hits him with a left hook into the other side of his opponent. Kellan grunts in pain and slowly leans over, Atlas slowly twists his body to the outside. As he cocks his fist back in preparation for delivering an overhand punch to the back of Kellan's head, Kellan says, "Your friend Geo was scum."

Atlas feels a power surge into his body as he remembers the pain that all of the people that he knows have experienced, and delivers a vicious blow to knock out Kellan.

As Atlas slowly stands back up from hitting Kellan,

he starts to glow a bright white that fills the entire arena. Leonel scrambles to put up multiple force fields in preparation for what is coming for him. Atlas looks at Leonel, and almost instantaneously it seems, flash to the force fields that were about 30 yards away. Atlas throws a single punch, transferring the momentum from running into it, that breaks through all 8 of Leonel's force fields and connects with Leonel's face and incapacitates him.

The white light begins to dim as Atlas hears, "WE WON THE SERIES 2-1," over the speakers by the now free Mrs. Brown and his friends that have all come to. He slowly smiles as he sees the faces of all of his friends that have regained consciousness as he looks up at the skybox and then drops down to the ground with tears of pain and joy running down his face.

∞∞∞∞

As the members from The End begin to get in the cylinder that would transport them back to the base, Mrs. Brown begins to talk.

"Thank you guys," she says to the students that were part of The End as she walks into the room with them "I know that it was a lot and that I don't have any room to talk as you guys were brought into this unwillingly. I still just want to say that I am genuinely sorry for the loss of your friends. I never could have imagined that any of those events would happen."

"But it did and that's the thing. They are gone. They

did die. They can't come back. And this is all on you," says Zev as tears continue to run down his face like the steady stream of a river.

"I'm so-," says Mrs. Brown before Atlas tells her to stop talking.

"I'll take this," says Atlas as he wraps his arm around Zev and turns him around.

Mrs. Brown leaves the room filled with all of the students crying heavier than she's ever witnessed anybody cry before.

"It'll be okay guys, we will get through this. Loss is something that happens in life no matter what, and we have to learn to understand and accept that. We can't take it out on people that had no say or role in the outcome of events. I understand you guys' pain, and I'll be here as we all must get through this together," says Atlas as his Awoken mark begins to glow as he smiles through the pain for his friends, helping them to smile and be distracted from what has happened. They all begin to talk about their future and all that they want to do in life to change the world while they prepare to go home. Atlas holds back the tears from all of the pain that he is bearing for the others, and even bears the pain of his opponents in the previous matches.

Chapter 15

2:48 AM Thursday May 13th, 2117

"Mrs. Brown. When I felt the pain of all of the members of The Beginning and The End, during the final mission, I felt strong feelings of pain. I felt pain coming from countless scenarios: loss of a loved one because they didn't have the funds to afford the medical bills; betrayal by someone that you put the utmost faith in and made yourself vulnerable to; feeling like your voice isn't being heard in a government that is meant to help everyone; not being able to take advantage of opportunities and education because of your parents' financial state; not being able to provide for your family even when you work a 40+ hour work week; losing a person that you care about; the government not caring for the people that care for the sick; never being able to find joy in life as they had to grow up too fast, and I can go on and on Mrs. President. However since you are going to be involved in the government, behind the scenes after everything that has happened I presume, I need you to do something about everybody's struggles. It may not be possible to take everyone's pain away all on your own instantly, and I know that, but I will help in any way that I can. I need you to do this as well. I need you to develop policies and programs to help build and protect the youth at all different class levels. I need you to do everything that you can to make sure that everybody is set in this world, no matter their race, gender, financial situation, or where they come from. It shouldn't matter. None of those things should matter. Everyone should be able to live a life with a joyful youth, prosperous adulthood, and thrive in a world where pain isn't ignored because someone is different than the majority whether it be race or financial situation or where someone lives," says Atlas as he speaks to the voice mailbox of Mrs. Brown while he lays in his bed staring at the ceiling again. "Once everyone understands that everyone can feel pain and suffer just as they do, the world will become a much more caring, and kind place," says Atlas as he thinks about how to achieve his dream for the world.

Atlas is trying to recover from the recent events and deal with the pain, agony, and losses that he suffered. He wants to take everyone's pain away. He decides that he will find a way to use his Awoken power on every person in the world, no matter how hard it may be for himself, so that he can cut the string that haunts everybody the same...pain. He plans to work on a small scale, and then widen his sphere of impact as he continues to empathize, sympathize, and understand the pain of everyone that he encounters while traveling the country. Atlas decides to try and bear the burden of pain for everybody as he does his best to make an impact on every person's life that he encounters by understanding their pain no matter what. He hopes to try and string together the teardrops of pain that connect everybody.

∞∞∞

As both Mrs. Thema Brown and Ade both sit in a room in a penthouse in South Africa, Mrs. Brown says to Ade," Well, that went well."

"It sure did Mrs. Brown," replies Ade. "Next time let's pick more even teams for the showdown."

"They were even. My team was just better than yours was all," replies Mrs. Brown.

"Well I think that that was the first and last time that I will ever pull a stunt like that," says Mrs. Brown as she lets out a sigh. "I think I'm gonna try and fix society the right way now though. By thinking of how everything I do affects everyone. It's not just us in the world. We can't just toy with the lives of people simply because we have power and influence in this world," continues Mrs. Brown.

"Excuse me, what was that?" asks Ade.

Mrs. Brown replies by saying, "You heard me."

"I know, I know. But hold on a second, how are you gonna fake your death, deceive the world, and then try and fix the same world that you just deceived?" asks Ade.

"I don't know myself, but once I understood the levels to which pain is rooted because of that boy, I felt like I had to do something. I know I was wrong in the past, and I thought I had it all figured out, but I didn't, I still don't. I haven't been thinking of everyone. It kind of seems like nobody does really… but pain… pain really is what connects us all. I had these big dreams growing up and wanted to make everyone happy, but I wasn't thinking of everybody. I was only thinking of what would make me look good. I just tried to follow what I've seen past Presidents do. I wanted to help every-one, but for that, you have to sacrifice and carry some of the burden yourself as well. That is what that boy taught me," says Mrs. Brown as a tear runs down her face. "Well maybe you'll understand it too one day Ade. Hopefully you aren't as stubborn as you were when we were growing up though. You have to be able to accept your past mistakes and grow. Make up for what you did wrong ten-fold. I'd get as upset as mom used to be right now if you didn't start to do that. At least try. Do it for mom," says Mrs. Brown while looking out the full glass window.

"Maybe I will one day. I do know the feeling of pain though," says Ade as he sheds a tear. "I wonder what Mom is doing up there", says Ade as he looks out the glass window at the stars above the beautiful cityscape of South Africa.

"Yeah Ade, me too", replies Mrs. Brown.

∞∞∞

The End

About The Author

Jeremiah Pouncy

My name is Jeremiah Pouncy and I am a 19 year old, African American male living in America. Growing up very fortunate. I have both of my loving parents, and two younger siblings that have always looked up to me. They all taught and encouraged me to dream big, care for others with everything in me, and to never give up so that I can achieve my goals and dreams.

I aspire to be an Exotic Animal Veterinarian. I will graduate from the illustrious North Carolina Agricultural and Technical State University (NC A&T), and continue my journey to Vet School. I will eventually open my own Exotic Animal Veterinary practice, and then develop it into a multi-million dollar business. I desire to spread the importance of education to young black children in developing countries, and to the less fortunate minority. This will allow the upcoming generations to have their mind set on getting an education and following through with their plans. I truly hope to inspire young black youth and adults, and to become someone that people can look up to teaching them that whatever they set their mind to, they can achieve.

Message From The Author

To be able to bear the pain of others is a draining and difficult thing for anyone to do on their own. Nobody has superpowers or Awoken Abilities in the real world. Though I wish that there were people with superpowers, there are not. To be able to come together and understand one another in the world today is something that needs to be achieved. Politicians should really think of everyone, especially the people that are struggling at the bottom of society; people that also feel pain and emotion, this is what the world needs. We as people must be able to understand the pain of others. For the people, we should be able to hold the weight of their pain no matter what tasks in life we are over. We must share the weight of the world rather than push the powerless and less fortunate even further down, how about lift them up. Instead of neglecting the lower class, the people who do the jobs that are required for a society to flourish, the jobs that require so much sacrifice and time, why don't we build them up and truly understand their situations? Why don't the minority communities, that have been oppressed by systematic racism and implicit bias, have anyone to lean on? Why are they still struggling, but the rich are getting richer? We have to be there for each other to lean on no matter what. We should find the will to take care of those that are experiencing pain by sacrificing something of ourselves for the greater good of everybody. When everyone comes together and shares the inevitable pain that life brings, the world will become a better place.

Made in the USA
Coppell, TX
26 September 2020

38835203R00066